Our City

OUR CITY

Julie Bertagna   Cathy Cassidy

John Fardell   Alison Flett

Vivian French   Keith Gray

Elizabeth Laird   Jonathan Meres

Nicola Morgan   Alison Prince

Foreword by
Rt Hon. George Grubb

Introduction by
James Mackenzie, BBC's 'Raven'

Illustrations by
John Fardell

First published in
Great Britain in 2008 by
Polygon, an imprint of Birlinn Ltd
West Newington House
10 Newington Road
Edinburgh
EH9 1QS

9 8 7 6 5 4 3 2 1

www.birlinn.co.uk

The publisher wishes to acknowledge
help with this publication from

·EDINBVRGH·
THE CITY OF EDINBURGH COUNCIL

edinburgh
(edɪnbʌrə) n.
UNESCO City of
Literature

ISBN 978 1 84697 090 0

British Library Cataloguing-in-Publication Data
A catalogue record for this book is available on
request from the British Library.

Typeset by Antony Gray
Printed and bound by Clays Ltd, St Ives plc

Contents

Foreword 7

Introduction 9

All Change *Jonathan Meres* 13

The Water Fight *Elizabeth Laird* 31

Red-handed *Keith Gray* 49

The Music Shop *John Fardell* 61

Word of Crow *Vivian French* 63

The Storyteller *Alison Flett* 82

The Smile *Alison Prince* 105

Friends Forever *Cathy Cassidy* 130

The Portobello Piper *Julie Bertagna* 143

The Boy With No Name *Nicola Morgan* 157

Authors' Biographies 179

Foreword

Welcome to *Our City*, the second book to be published in support of the OneCity Trust. This is a unique project, which brings together ten of Scotland's best children's writers, with new, specially written stories. All the stories here are set in Edinburgh: some in its familiar streets, and some in fantastical, futuristic, and comic versions of the city.

I have always been proud to be part of Edinburgh, to serve it, and to call it my home: it is a place of immense beauty and inspiration, cultural significance and historical importance, and is now the fourth largest financial centre in Europe. But there is another Edinburgh too: one in which, today, 4,500 people are homeless; where one in 48 elderly people die of poverty; where nearly half of adults to the north of the city have no qualifications, and where too many children grow up in families with no income. The OneCity Trust is committed to empowering communities in tackling these divisions, by supporting grassroots projects which address inequality and exclusion, so that the great benefits of Edinburgh can be enjoyed by all.

I thank the authors, who responded to our request for

stories with such warm generosity and imagination, and whose goodwill, in donating their royalties, will enable the work of the Trust to continue to grow. And my heartfelt thanks go to you, for buying this book, and making it possible.

But books are nothing without readers, and *Our City* is for savouring, sharing, and reading aloud. Almost all of Edinburgh is here: I hope you enjoy it.

Rt Hon. George Grubb
Lord Provost of Edinburgh

Find out more about the work of the Trust at
www.onecity.org.uk

Introduction

JAMES MACKENZIE, BBC'S 'RAVEN'

My earliest memories of Edinburgh are of being in the theatre with my dad. He is an actor, and, if he was doing a show, I'd come through with him from West Lothian where we lived. I used to hang out backstage and watch the rehearsals – I even got to go to the opening night parties! I didn't want to be an actor to begin with, though: what I really wanted to do when I grew up was drive a lorry.

Then, when I was eight, I started going to West Lothian Youth Theatre. I loved it, because it wasn't about learning to be a great actor: it was about having the freedom to use your imagination and learning to be confident in yourself. There were kids there from all sorts of backgrounds, and it didn't matter if you were good at acting or not – it was just fun. My favourite thing was improvisation, where you make up your own story and act it out as you go along. I used to write stories too, and draw pictures to make them into comic strips, but I was rubbish at drawing, so all the superheroes were just stick men.

Stories were a really big part of my childhood. I was incredibly lucky to have parents who read books to me: they used to read Dickens and *Lord of the Rings* and *The Hobbit*, and do all the different voices. Of course, Dad was a professional, so it was pretty special! I think there's something magical about having a story read to you: it's not like watching TV, where all you have to do is take in what's on the screen. When you're listening to a story, you have to picture it in your own mind, and doing that takes you into a different world. At the moment, I'm reading all the James Bond books, because I love the way everything is described: all the exotic places, the food, the clothes and the cars. It's really exciting to be able to see these things in your own head while you're reading, and imagine being there yourself.

But now I'm a character in a story too! When I decided that I wanted to be an actor after all, I moved to Edinburgh to study drama at Queen Margaret's – and 'Raven' was my first big TV job after college. It was pretty weird. One day I was James, going to the shop for some milk, and the next day I was this heroic, half-man/half-bird creature, dressed in black feathers, zapping people and having fights with baddies!

'Raven' is basically about good and evil, like all the classic stories. Raven lived in a mythical land called Alaunus, which was a land of peace until a character called Nevar turned bad and decided to try and take over. Nevar is a real villain – his whole aim in life is to rule the world with his evil demons. Raven's quest is to find young warriors and teach them his ways, so that they can champion the forces of good and protect his land from Nevar. The TV show is all about the challenges that Raven sets for the teams, who compete to be the Ultimate Warrior.

Being Raven is fantastic, but it's the young warriors who are the real stars. They all put so much into it – and it can be pretty scary, to come to a remote place in Scotland, or even India, and take part in really difficult mental and physical challenges, with people you've never met before. But the best thing is that once you're in your costume and playing your warrior role, it doesn't matter where you come from, whether you're rich or poor, or a goth or a geek, or whether or not you're good at school – everyone's equal, and it's about who you are inside, and what you can achieve.

For me, the most important thing in life is the freedom to be yourself, to get out and do things, to use your imagination and choose your own future. People talk about 'social inclusion' – it's what this book is in aid of – but I think that often the people who talk about it don't have a clue what it's like not to have that freedom. I still live in the flat in Leith that I had when I first moved to Edinburgh as a student, and things have changed a lot over the years. There are all the new flats along the Shore, and trendy new bars and restaurants, and people with more money. But, in Leith, you can never forget that life's different on the other side of the street, and it's one of the things that make it a really special place. Edinburgh has great wealth, and also great poverty – but visitors don't often see the other side, because most of it is hidden away, on the edges of the city. The OneCity Trust works hard to make people aware of how difficult things are for many families in Edinburgh and finds ways of helping – and you are helping too, by reading this book.

I'm really glad I was asked to write the introduction to *Our City*, because I know how lucky I am to have the life I do – and also because I know how powerful stories can be. There are magical stories here, and stories which are funny and sad, scary and exciting. These stories are all about Edinburgh and full of people and places we recognise. You might even recognise yourself in some of them! But they also take us into other places – surprising new worlds that might make us see ourselves and others differently.

Enjoy, brave warriors!

James Mackenzie
Edinburgh

12

All Change

JONATHAN MERES

There's just something about the number 15 I really like. Not that I actually *dislike* any of the other numbers. I've got nothing against those guys at all. It's nothing personal. The 44 . . . the 31 . . . the 8 . . . the 26 . . . the 11. They're perfectly *nice* numbers. It's just that . . . I don't know. There's just something about the number 15 that makes it *special*, that's all. Something that makes it, well, just different I suppose. I can't explain.

I think the colour's probably got something to do with it. Proper red. Not something in between. Not some *shade* of red that can't seem to make up its mind and has to have some stupid name, like Moroccan Kiss, or Sunset Blaze. No – the number 15 is just plain red. Like a Christmas card robin's breast, or one of those telephone boxes from the olden days like that guy round the corner's got in his garden.

Then again, perhaps it's not so much the actual shade of red, as the way it contrasts with the crisp white roof and the horizontal stripe separating the upper and lower decks. Simple but classy. Unlike some of the other routes, with their fancy colour schemes and random patterns, which can be confusing, if you're not an expert like me. No problem with the number 15 though. You can spot a number 15 a mile away. Or 1.6 kilometres if you prefer. There's simply no mistaking it for any other bus.

'Well?' says my dad. 'Are you going to get on, or just stare at it all day?'

'Yeah, come on Greg you geek,' says my brother. 'Some of us have actually *got* a life you know!'

'Now, now, Jordan, there's no need for that,' says my mum.

'Well he *is* a geek,' says Jordan.

'You heard your mother. That's enough!' says my dad.

'But . . .'

'No buts, Jordan. I said that's enough, do you hear?'

Meanwhile, as the debate about whether or not I'm a geek is raging, the bus driver has started the engine and opened the door.

'Are you sure you don't want us to just drive you there, love?' says my mum. 'It'd be a lot quicker you know.'

Mum's smiling this soppy kind of smile at me, so I smile back. She means well, my mum.

'It's OK thanks, Mum,' I say. 'I want to do it.'

Which is true, by the way. I really *do* want to do it. I've never done it before. Not by myself anyway. There was that time with Grandpa of course. But I've never done it alone. And I want to. I've got to. I *need* to. It could be character-building. But even if it's not, I still want to do it. I don't say anything though, because Jordan will probably call me a geek again and then there'll be trouble. And anyway, the bus is about to leave and I really should get on.

Mum says something, but I don't hear what, because I've been thinking all that stuff.

'Pardon, Mum?'

'I said, will you call us when you get there?'

'Course I will, Mum.'

'We'll come and pick you up in the morning,' says my dad.

'Geek,' says Jordan, under his breath so that only I hear him.

Mum gives me a kiss on my cheek. Dad ruffles my hair. I get on the bus.

'Where to, pal?' says the driver.

I don't know why he bothers asking. It's one fare, any distance. Perhaps he's just making polite conversation.

'All the way please,' I say, trying to sound like it's not my first time and that it's not a particularly big deal, even though it *is* both of those things.

'60p, pal,' says the driver, like I didn't know that already.

I must look my age though, otherwise he would have said 'a pound, pal'. 60p is a child fare and child fares apply between the ages of five and fifteen. And I'm exactly halfway between five and fifteen.

Mum and Dad had this big debate about whether ten was old enough to be doing a journey like this all by myself. I know they did, because I heard them when I came into the kitchen this morning. They stopped when they saw me though, like they were discussing something embarrassing that I shouldn't be listening to. But it's not embarrassing. It's just a bus journey.

Dad said something about biking to North Berwick when he was my age, and that was before mobile phones. I said, 'Dad, that was before *phones*, not just *mobile* phones,' but he knew I was only joking. Then Mum looked at me and said, 'What do *you* think, Greg? Do *you* think ten's old enough to be doing this?' Like I'm going to turn round and say, 'Actually Mum, no I don't, can you take me by car instead please?' Honestly, what is she like?

Anyway, I pay my 60p and take my ticket, then climb the stairs and sit down at the front on the right hand side. It's where I always sit if I've got a choice. And I've got plenty of choice today. I'm the only one on the bus. We pull away almost immediately. I look out the window and see  my mum and dad waving at me. I wave back. Jordan pulls a face.

This is it then. We're off. Well, *I'm* off anyway. Mum

and Dad and Jordan get smaller, then disappear as we turn a corner.

*

Grandpa bought my ticket for me last time. I can remember it like it was yesterday. It wasn't, obviously. It was a few months ago. But it seems like yesterday.

'Here,' he said, handing it to me. 'You can pay me back later.'

I laughed.

'What's so funny?'

'You always say that, Grandpa! But I never do!'

'Aye, well,' said Grandpa, tapping the side of his head with one finger. 'It's all up here, don't you worry. I'm keeping count. I'm not losing my marbles *just* yet!'

Grandpa? Lose his marbles? That'll be the day, I thought to myself. He was as fit as a fiddle, not like some of the old folk you saw. Not that Grandpa was *that* old. He wasn't even bald!

'About time we did this,' said Grandpa, gazing out the window.

'I know,' I said.

There was nothing more to say. It *was* about time we actually *went* on a number 15, instead of just staring whenever one passed by. There'd just never been an opportunity until now. Dad had always driven me to Grandma and Grandpa's whenever I'd gone to stay before. But, that time, Dad was away and Mum couldn't give me a lift because Jordan had got football or something. Anyway, Grandpa had come over specially and now here we were, sat at the front on the right hand side. And not just for part of the route either. The whole route, from start to finish. In a oner.

Some route it was too. One of Lothian Buses' longest, maybe even *the* longest. Tranent to Penicuik and back again. Twenty-four miles each way. Or 38.6 kilometres if you prefer. Starting and finishing in the countryside. Slap bang through the centre of Edinburgh in the middle. Roughly L-shaped on the map, depending on which way you looked at it. An hour and forty minutes, depending on traffic.

The bus stopped to pick up a woman talking on her phone, and a few seconds later she appeared upstairs, still talking, and sat down halfway back on the other side. I could see her reflection in the curved round mirror above me. But the mirror wasn't there for my benefit. It was there for the driver, so he could check for any sign of trouble on the top deck, by looking into a special kind of periscope thing.

There'd been trouble once. I think it might have been on a 14 going to Newhaven. Or was it a 12 going to the zoo? Anyway, the driver had to stop and come upstairs because a guy was chucking chips about and someone had complained. One hit Grandpa on the back of his head. Grandpa just turned round and told the guy could he make sure there was ketchup next time?

That was one thing I liked about Grandpa. He didn't say much, but what he did say was usually funny, or true. Quite often it was funny *and* true. But he definitely didn't waste words, Grandpa. It was almost like there was some kind of rule. You know, like he was only actually *allowed* to say so many words each day, and once he'd reached that limit he couldn't say anything else? Yeah, that's what it was like.

There were loads of other things I liked about Grandpa too – things that made him not quite like normal grandpas. Not that there was anything *wrong* with the normal kind of grandpa: the kind that wears a cardigan, and smiles all the time, and dishes out sweets and pointless advice. Grandpa only ever gave you a sweet if it was one he didn't like! And the only advice he ever gave me was never to listen to advice, but I think he might have been joking. He had a strange sense of humour, Grandpa. Some people didn't understand him, but I did. He was just different, that's all. A bit like the number 15 bus.

Grandpa liked buses too. In fact it was Grandpa who got me into buses in the first place. It certainly wasn't Dad or Jordan! They just didn't get it at all. Dad said the bus thing must have skipped a generation, which made it sound like some kind of hideous, incurable disease.

At least my family never teased me. OK, so Jordan called me a geek, but I didn't mind that. And anyway, he didn't mean it. Not like some of the kids at school, who treated me like I was a total weirdo just because I wasn't into the same things as them. Like football and . . . well, football basically.

I didn't care, though. As far as I was concerned it was them who were weird, not me. And anyway, I'd be moving to high school soon. It was going to be like starting out all over again. There'd be new kids from all the other primaries. Maybe one of them might even like buses too! We could be bus buddies! But even if there wasn't anybody else who liked buses, I still didn't care. I like them, and that's that.

Not just *any* old buses, by the way. It has to be *Lothian* buses. I don't know why – it's just one of those things. How can you explain an obsession? Not that I'm obsessed. Oh all right then, maybe I am. Just a wee bit. But so what? I don't care. I honestly don't care!

'Oystercatchers,' said Grandpa.

'What?' I said.

'Oystercatchers,' said Grandpa again.

I looked out the window. We'd stopped next to Mussel-burgh Racecourse to pick up a man and a woman with a baby in a buggy. A bunch of birds stood on the grass, all pointing in the same direction. There must have been a hundred of them, all completely still, like soldiers on parade. Black and white, with long straight orange beaks. All exactly the same. All except one. One single bird, slap bang in the middle, pointing the opposite way. It was bigger, and brown, with this huge long beak curving down.

It was me! The bird pointing the other way was me! The rest of them – the oystercatchers – were the football-loving kids at school, all the same in their identical strips. But the brown one was me! What's that word, where one thing represents another?

'Curlew,' said Grandpa, as the bus pulled away again.

'What?' I said.

'Curlew,' said Grandpa. 'The brown one with the long curved bill. It's a curlew.'

'Right,' I said.

That was another thing I liked about Grandpa. He always knew what was going on in my head. He seemed to *understand* me better than anyone else. Better than Jordan. Better than Mum and Dad. Better than me, even!

Why was that? I wondered. Did Grandpa actually have some kind of amazing mind-reading powers?

'I know what you're thinking,' said Grandpa.

I couldn't believe it. This was beginning to get freaky.

'What?' I said. 'Really?'

Grandpa turned and looked at me for a moment.

'Nah, not really,' he said. 'I was just kidding.'

Before long we'd left Musselburgh and were rumbling along the road to Joppa. We were just a stone's throw from the sparkling waters of the Firth of Forth. Well, if you were good at throwing stones we were. Which I'm not. And even if I was, I personally wouldn't recommend throwing stones from the top deck of a number 15 bus. Or any other bus for that matter. The driver would see you through the periscope thing, and you might get thrown off. Oh, and when I said '*sparkling* waters of the Firth of Forth', I meant *for now* they were sparkling. They're not always.

Out in the middle of the firth I could see a huge tanker, and across on the other side something glinted as the sun reflected off it.

'If you can see Fife it's gonnae rain,' said Grandpa, putting on a funny high voice and deliberately exaggerating his accent.

It was my turn.

'If you cannae see Fife it's raining already,' I said, putting on a funny voice of my own.

Grandpa and I looked at each other and grinned. Well, *I* did. Grandpa *nearly* grinned.

Sure enough, before we were even halfway along Portobello High Street, the sky had turned grey. By the time the bus started the gradual climb away from the firth and towards the city, the first drops of rain had already begun to fall.

I could see another 15 coming towards us from the opposite direction.

'366,' I said in a flash.

'368,' said Grandpa.

It was our game: Guess The Fleet Number. Not the *route* number – that's easy. The actual *fleet* number is different on every bus. In the case of the number 15, there were only nine to choose from, so there was always a fair chance one of us would win.

Not this time, though.

'367,' I said, as the two buses passed each other.

'Close,' said Grandpa.

A few minutes later we passed Meadowbank Stadium which, as far as I could tell, wasn't near a meadow *or* a bank. What were they thinking? Mind you, Arthur's Seat doesn't look much like a chair. So fair enough, I suppose.

As we got closer to the city centre, the bus started to fill up. There were eight or nine others on the top deck by now, including a guy with a ponytail reading a book and a couple of teenage girls at the back, giggling. The woman with the mobile was *still* talking. She hadn't stopped since she'd got on! I couldn't imagine what someone could find to talk about all that time. Me and Grandpa had hardly spoken. But then we hardly needed to.

We were coming up to the roundabout where London Road meets Leith Walk. Getting closer to the best shop in the world: Harburn Hobbies. Well, the best shop in the world if you're into model planes and trains and cars. Or in my case, buses. I don't suppose it's that great if you're not. I'd got a pretty good collection of Lothian buses already, lined up on a shelf in my room. The 21 . . . the 22 . . . the 25 . . . the 37 . . . the X50 to the *Britannia*. The *big* news was they were bringing out a number 15 soon. Not soon enough for me, though!

We slowed to a halt. I could almost *see* Harburn Hobbies. It was now or never.

'Er, Grandpa?' I said.

'Not today, Greg,' said Grandpa straight away.

I knew it. I just knew he'd know what I was thinking.

'Yeah but . . .'

'No buts, Greg.'

I sighed. I knew better than to argue with Grandpa, but I decided to give it one last shot anyway.

'We could just nip in quickly and then get the *next* one. Or the one after that. We wouldn't have to wait long.'

'Grandma's expecting us. She'll have tea ready. It's your favourite.'

'Macaroni cheese?'

Grandpa nodded.

'Garlic bread?'

Another nod.

I sighed again. Grandpa drove a hard bargain. I'd just have to be patient. We could go next time.

We eventually pulled away again, heading up the hill and past the Playhouse. On the steps of the cathedral, clusters of darkly dressed people stood chatting in the rain. It looked like there'd been a funeral. I glanced at Grandpa to see if he'd noticed, but his eyes were closed.

'Grandpa?' I said, as casually as possible.

'What?'

'Are you OK?'

'Why wouldn't I be?'

'Were you asleep?'

'Just checking the inside of my eyelids.'

'Look,' I said, pointing ahead.

Grandpa looked. Another 15 was approaching from the opposite direction.

'370,' I said.

'Correct,' said Grandpa, and closed his eyes again.

As we slowed to a halt in St Andrew Square, the woman talking on her mobile suddenly jumped up and started waving to someone out the window. I could see her in the mirror. Everyone could *hear* her.

'I'm on the top deck!' she shouted. 'Over here!'

Down on the pavement below, another woman on a mobile looked up and started waving back frantically. A few seconds later, the woman appeared at the top of the stairs, made her way down the aisle, and sat next to her friend. Only *then* did they finally put their phones down. I couldn't understand it. They'd been *talking* to each other even though they were just about to *see* each other. Bizarre.

'You'd think they could have waited,' I said.

'Aye,' said Grandpa.

'Whatever they were talking about must've been very important.'

Grandpa looked in the mirror.

'Or maybe not,' he said.

I looked in the mirror too. The two women were sat, staring out the window and not saying a word.

We turned right on to Princes Street. The rain had stopped. Well, for the time being it had, anyway. It was still quite dark though, and the Scott Monument loomed above us, like some kind of Victorian space rocket ready for blast-off. In the distance stood the castle, keeping watch over the city, just as it had done since . . . since . . . well, since ages ago, basically.

Loads of tourists got on at the next stop, and came up to the top deck so they could take photos. But all I wanted to look at now was buses. And Princes Street was bus heaven! In fact there was practically nothing *but* buses on Princes Street. Most of the Lothian routes meet up here, as if they're attracted by some massive magnet, or drawn along by some kind of conveyor belt, like a real life Scalextric set. It's brilliant! Well, if you're into buses it is, anyway. I don't suppose it's that brilliant if you're not.

Before I knew it we'd turned left and were heading past the Caledonian Hotel, where Grandpa worked when he was young, washing dishes. He said it was the best job he ever had, not because he particularly liked washing dishes or anything, but because he met Grandma! Grandma was working there too. They'd go dancing afterwards at this place just down the road and they saw The Beatles once, who were like this dead famous pop group. I've seen the photos. They looked so happy. Grandma and Grandpa, I mean. Not The Beatles.

By now the traffic was really heavy. The two women with the mobiles had got off, but I hadn't noticed when. And as if by magic, the girls on the back seat had also disappeared and been replaced by a group of teenage boys listening to music on their phones and shouting at people out the window. The guy with the book and the ponytail was still there though, but all of a sudden he looked up and ran downstairs.

'Holy Corner,' said Grandpa, out of the blue.

'Pardon?' I said, wondering whether this was one of those funny expressions Grandpa came out with occasionally, like 'Gordon Bennet', or 'My giddy aunt'.

'Holy Corner,' said Grandpa again.

We'd stopped at a junction.

'See? Church on each corner,' said Grandpa. 'Holy Corner.'

'Right,' I said, wondering how Grandpa knew all this

stuff. Stuff about birds? Stuff about places? Perhaps it was just that the older you got, the more stuff you learnt. Not that Grandpa was old, of course. He still played golf and kicked a ball about in the back garden with Jordan. He could even do keepie-uppies!

*

The next thing I know, my mouth's all dry and my neck's stiff from resting my head against the window. I open my eyes. I don't remember falling asleep. But then I don't suppose you ever do.

Outside, it's started to rain again. Well, I mean *obviously* outside. It's hardly likely to rain *inside*, is it?

We're coming into Penicuik. Grandma's going to be there to meet me. At least I hope she is. I look in the mirror. There's no one else on the top deck. Everyone's got off. I'm all alone. Just like Grandma.

I'm not going to be sad though. I've decided. Even though this is going to be the first time I've been to Grandma's since Grandpa died. Even though everyone keeps saying it's OK to be sad. I *know* it's OK to be sad. It's just that, well, I'll be sad when I *want* to be sad, not when I'm told to be. Right now, I'm going to be strong for Grandma. It's only been a few weeks. She's still getting used to things the way they are now. So I'm going to make myself useful and do loads of jobs round the house and stuff. Like Grandpa would have wanted me to.

We pass a massive school and I think of the school I'll be going to after the summer holidays. I think of the single curlew in amongst all the oystercatchers. I think of Grandpa knowing exactly what I'm thinking. And thinking *that* makes me grin. Which makes me think of Grandpa *nearly* grinning. Which makes me grin even more.

Which reminds me. I never did pay Grandpa back for the ticket.

Anyway, while I've been thinking all that stuff, the bus has stopped and I suddenly realise. I've done it. The whole journey. In a oner. All by myself.

'All change!' shouts the driver up the stairs. And he's right. Because that's exactly what it feels like. All change.

But he doesn't mean that. He means it's time to get off the bus. And when I do, Grandma's waiting for me. I knew she would be.

'Here. I've got something for you,' she says, handing me a yellow plastic bag.

I take the bag and look at it.

'Harburn Hobbies,' it says, in black lettering.

I open it. There, in a box, is a bus. Not just any bus. A Lothian bus. Not just any Lothian bus. A number 15. Red, with a white roof and a white stripe separating the upper and lower decks. Not just any red. Proper red.

I try to say something. But I can't.

Grandma smiles.

'Your favourite for tea, love.'

'Macaroni cheese?' I say.
Grandma nods.
'Garlic bread?'
She nods again.
Some things never change.

The Water Fight

ELIZABETH LAIRD

Have you ever moved house? No? Then don't. It's a nightmare. You have to pack up every single thing you've got. Clear out all your shelves. Stop your mum throwing all your collections away.

The worst bit is saying goodbye to everything. To the people in your street. To your friends at school. To the cat on the wall near the corner shop. And the place by the swings where you always met your mates.

The next worst thing is that everyone gets tired and fed up. Especially your mum. And your dad does too, probably. I wouldn't know about that. My dad's not around much. He's on the rigs most of the time.

Take it from me, I know what I'm talking about. We've moved loads of times. Hundreds of times, probably. You have to, when your dad's on the rigs. And I hate it.

This last time was the worst of all. I had a great gang of friends in our old place. Darren, and Neil, and Ahmed. And I didn't know anyone around here. Not a single person.

It was scorching hot the day we moved. Everything was boiling. If you touched a piece of metal, your fingers began to fry. If you went out into the sun, your hair almost caught fire.

'I can't believe it,' Mum kept saying. 'It's the tropics up here. More like Delhi than Edinburgh. Global warming, I suppose.'

It was miles and miles from our old place in Restalrig to this house out in Juniper Green. We arrived at exactly the same moment as the furniture van. I didn't even have time to go indoors and take a proper look around.

'Here, carry this in for me,' Mum said. She was already putting a massive box into my arms. 'Find the kitchen and put it down on the floor. Carefully, mind.'

For the next hour we didn't stop. It was in and out, backwards and forwards, up the stairs and down again.

Sometimes, I rested for a minute and tried to catch my breath.

'Jamie!' Mum would yell at me, every time. 'Take this mirror up to my bedroom. Jamie! Put this chair in the sitting room. And watch out for the paintwork. It's new.'

Suddenly, I'd had enough. I marched into the kitchen, pulled back the bolts on the back door and opened it. Then I went out into the garden.

That garden was a proper jungle. There was a bit of grass in the middle, really long, like in a field. There might have been flowers and stuff round the edge of it once, but there were just masses of weeds now. They'd grown so tall they were almost over my head.

It was only a tiddly wee garden, but there was a tree at the bottom, a nice old apple tree. There were apples on it too. Not big enough to eat yet, though.

It was shady under the tree. I flopped down onto the grass and leaned against the trunk. I could hear Mum yelling, 'Jamie! Where are you? Come here! Jamie!'

I put my hands over my ears. To be quite honest, I wanted to cry. We'd only left our old house a few hours ago, but I was dying of homesickness already.

'I hate it here. I *hate* it!' I muttered to myself.

I wanted to stand up, go through the house, out onto the road, turn left and run all the way down the Lanark Road, march past Haymarket, and go on and on down to Leith. I wouldn't stop until I was at home again.

But I knew I couldn't. Someone else was in our house

in our old close now. Another family. They were stupid and mean, I just knew they were. Even if I found my way there, they'd never let me in.

When I thought of other people, mucking about in my old bedroom, I had to give a gigantic sniff. Well, two or three, if you must know.

Then I realised that I wasn't quite alone.

There was a thin patch in the weeds beside the fence on one side. And through a gap in the wooden slats I could see a flash of yellow. It was moving. It looked like a skirt or a dress or something. With someone inside it.

I sat very still and tried to make myself small. I wasn't ready to meet the neighbours yet. I didn't ever want to meet them, anyway. I knew I wasn't going to like them.

The yellow skirt disappeared and then I saw a blob of pink in its place. It was a face. Someone was bending down and staring at me through the gap in the fence. I could see a shiny eye, big and round, not even blinking.

'You're crying,' a girl's voice said suddenly.

I wiped my cheeks furiously with the back of my hand.

'I'm not. It's hay fever. And sweat. That's all.'

The face disappeared, then I saw it again. The girl had stood up and was staring at me properly over the top of the fence.

I stared back. She was younger than me. Big, though. Her hair was pale and streaky and her skin was bright pink. She looked so hot I thought she was going to melt.

I wished she would.

'What are you doing in that garden?' she said. 'It's private. Private property.'

I didn't like her tone of voice.

'Aye. My private property,' I said. 'I live here.'

'Oh? Since when?'

'Since about two hours ago.'

'Oh. Have you got a dog?' She looked a bit more friendly all of a sudden.

'No.'

The friendly look vanished. She was still staring at me. I knew she could see I'd been crying. Well, sniffing, anyway.

'Like I said.' I was trying to sound cold and dignified. 'This is private property, and that includes people not staring at people over the fence.'

'Says who?' she said rudely.

'Says me.'

She didn't say anything for a moment, then she stuck her tongue out.

'You're a cry-baby. A silly wee cry-baby.'

'And you're – you're . . . '

I was trying to think of something really awful.

'You're a fat pig,' I said at last. 'Only you're not even a pig. You're just a piglet. The fattest piglet in the world.'

Her face went bright red. She opened her mouth to say something, but I could see she was too upset. Her eyes had gone wet and swimmy. Then she vanished.

One minute she was there, and the next minute she wasn't.

Oh great, I thought. Wonderful. I've only been here five minutes, and I've messed things up already.

I was a bit sorry for the girl now. Angry and sorry at the same time.

She started it, I told myself. She called me a cry-baby first.

I didn't know what to do. I stood there, under the apple tree, and all I could think was, Why doesn't everyone just leave me *alone*?

I had a good idea then. I decided to make a base. I'd burrow into the weedy, overgrown place behind the apple tree, and I'd make a good hideout for myself. It would be my place, just for me. I'd disappear into it whenever I liked. I'd be alone there, and no one would be able to get at me.

I walked over to the other side of the garden. It wasn't far. Only a few steps in fact. I could still hear the girl, snuffling away.

She's putting it on now, I thought, trying to convince myself. She just wants to make me feel bad.

There were a couple of big old bushes near the opposite fence. Weeds had grown up in front of them. They looked promising.

There'll be space inside that lot, I thought. I'll be able to make a proper hideout in there.

I bent down, parted the weeds, and looked inside. Then I got a shock.

Someone had made a base in there already. The earth had been trampled down. There were three rubbishy old chairs with the legs cut short, and a plank set up on bricks to make a table. There was an old football, two mugs with broken handles, and a jam jar with some dead flowers in it.

I crawled right in and had a good look round. There wasn't much room. The chairs and table took up more or less the whole space, and you couldn't stand up at all.

I sat down on one of the chairs and picked up the football. It was old and soft. It wouldn't be any good for a real game.

I was holding it in my hands, trying to balance it on one finger, when I heard voices. They were close, coming from just the other side of the fence.

And the next minute, there they were, two boys, about my age, crawling right into my new base behind me.

'Hey!' the younger one with the curly brown hair said. 'What are you doing with my football? Give it here.'

The other one, who looked older, was frowning so hard his eyes nearly disappeared under his big black eyebrows.

'This is our base,' he said. 'Who said you could come in?'

I felt a bit scared.

'And this is my garden,' I said. 'You're trespassing.'

We all glared at each other.

'Liar,' the older boy said at last. 'It can't be yours. No one's lived here for years.'

'Who are you calling a liar?' I was getting angry now. 'Go and look in the street. Never seen a removal van before?'

They looked at each other.

'This is our base, anyway,' the younger boy said, but he didn't sound so sure now.

'Not any more it isn't,' I said. I was starting to feel more confident. 'Make one in your own garden.'

The bigger boy started backing out again.

'Leave it, Greg,' he said. 'Come on out. This guy's a loser, anyway.'

I was furious now.

'Who are you calling a loser?' I yelled.

The bigger boy had already crawled away, but the younger one said, 'Give me back my football. I'm not going without my football.'

I don't know what got into me then. Maybe it was the heat, or being so angry and upset. I knew I wasn't being fair, but I said, 'No. It's in my garden, so it's mine now. Finders keepers.'

'Robbie! Did you hear that? He's nicked my football!' the boy called Greg shouted. He looked as if he was going to explode.

The other boy appeared again.

'You wee thief!' he said. 'Give Greg back his football.'

I looked from one to the other. There were two of them and only one of me. Anyway, I didn't feel angry any more. I just felt miserable.

'Take your stupid football then,' I said, throwing it at Robbie. 'It's rubbish, anyway.'

The next minute, they'd gone. I could hear them on the other side of the fence. They were yelling rude things, calling me the worst names they could think of.

I had to put my hands over my ears for the second time that day. I didn't feel like shouting back.

Nasty neighbours on both sides, I thought. That's it. This place is a hole. I hate it. I hate it. I *hate* it.

After a while, I couldn't hear Robbie and Greg any more. They must have gone inside. I could still hear the girl in the yellow dress though, bouncing a ball in her own garden. I crawled out of the base. It was a stupid place, anyway. There was nothing to do in there. Every time you moved, a sharp twig stuck in you. And it wasn't much fun, just sitting in there on my own.

I could hear Mum and the removal men, moving

around in the house. I wanted to go indoors, get myself a drink of something, and flop down on the sofa in front of the telly. But there weren't any cups or glasses out yet. They were still in the boxes. And the sofa was still in the van, and the telly wasn't connected up. Anyway, if I went indoors, Mum would start me working again.

I went back to the apple tree and sat down. There was nothing else to do.

Then I noticed something. A long, green thing was lying coiled up near the tree. It was half hidden by the long grass.

It gave me a fright, I can tell you. For one horrible moment, I thought it was a snake. Then I gave a sigh of relief. It was only a hosepipe.

It must have been there for years. The grass and weeds had grown right over it, and it looked all faded and rotten.

I bet it's full of holes, I thought. I picked up the end of it. A little bit of water trickled out. There must be a tap around here somewhere. Someone must have used this once to water the garden.

I went back up to the house. It was awful, coming out from the shade of the tree. The sun was so hot it made me feel dizzy.

I saw the tap at once. It was just under the kitchen window. And the hosepipe was still attached to it.

I reckoned it wouldn't work, but I switched it on anyway.

There was a whooshing sound. I looked round. Clear, sparkling water was gushing out of the other end of the hosepipe.

I felt like someone in a film, crossing a desert, who sees a river in the distance. I ran back to the apple tree, picked up the hose and splashed the water on my hands. It was great!

Then I turned it up towards my face. There was a gurgling noise in the hosepipe and a whole rush of water came out. It sprayed all over my face, into my eyes, up my nose and into my mouth.

It was terrific. I felt cooler now, and my head cleared. Suddenly, everything felt better.

I started shooting water all over the place. Down my legs. Onto my feet. Over my head. I was half soaked, but I didn't care.

Then I put one finger half over the end of the hose, to close up the hole and make the water come out faster. It was brilliant. It shot out in a lovely hard spray, and the sunlight got caught in it and made a rainbow.

I whooshed it all round the garden, hosing down the bushes, and the fence, and the apple tree.

'Oi! Mind what you're doing!'

It was the girl in the yellow dress again. She was standing up and glaring at me. Her hair was all wet and water was dripping off her face.

'Oops, sorry,' I said. 'I didn't know you were still there.'

I gave myself another squirt, under the chin, and squealed as the cold water ran down my neck.

The girl was looking at me enviously. Her face looked redder and hotter than ever.

'It's lovely,' I said. 'Really cool. Here, do you want a go?'

She shrugged.

'OK. Why not?'

I poked the end of the hose through the fence. She splashed herself carefully on her face, and her hands, and her bare feet.

'Thank you very much,' she said politely.

'No, you haven't had a proper go,' I said, and I lifted the hose, and squirted her full on.

It was risky, I know. She might have hated me forever. But I kind of knew she'd love it.

She did. She shrieked and ran about, and I kept squirting her, and she started laughing. It was great.

'Here, give it to me,' she said. 'It's my turn.'

'It doesn't reach that far,' I said, giving her a last splosh down the front.

'I'll come over then.'

She disappeared, and a moment later, there she was, standing beside me in my own garden.

'How did you get in?' I said, surprised.

'Easy. There's a hole in the fence. There's one on Robbie and Greg's side too. We often meet up in here. Your garden's nicer than ours. It's all wild.'

She grabbed the hose and started spraying me.

'Aagh!' I yelled. 'Oo! No! Stop!'

But I didn't want her to. It was great.

Then suddenly, she did stop. I was looking at her, and I could see this big grin on her face. She was pointing the hose away from me, towards the opposite side of the garden.

I spun round. Robbie and Greg were looking at us over the fence.

'You'd better watch it,' Robbie said, scowling. 'Don't you dare splash us.'

Greg was trying to look fierce too, but he only managed to look hot.

'What are you doing in there, Julie?' Greg said. 'You shouldn't be playing with him. Robbie says he's a loser.'

Julie didn't answer. She grabbed the hose out of my hand and began waving it around in the air.

'I'm going to make a rainbow,' she said. 'Look. Up there.'

She whirled it round. Water squirted over the fence and caught Robbie full in the face.

'Right! That's it!' he yelled.

He's going to come in here and get me, I thought. And he's big. And there are two of them.

But Greg had disappeared. A moment later, he was

back. And this time he had a great big water gun in his hands. He lifted it up and squirted it right at me. It got me on the only dry bit of me left, my tum. I gasped with the shock of it and staggered backwards. He was grinning. He knew he'd scored. There was only one thing I could do.

I grabbed the hose out of Julie's hand, and let him have it. The water caught him smack on the chest. The next shot from his gun hit me in the back. I slipped and fell flat on the grass. On the way down, I must have banged my elbow on the tree. Shoots of pain screamed up from my elbow to my shoulder. I lay there, stunned, with my eyes shut. I could see whirly lights in the blackness.

When I opened my eyes again, the three of them were looking down at me with worried faces.

'Are you OK?' said Robbie.

'You've gone a funny colour,' said Greg.

The pain was already starting to go away.

'You didn't bang your head, did you?' said Julie. 'You can kill yourself like that.'

I managed to sit up. My arm still hurt, but it wasn't too bad. The hose was lying beside me on the grass, and water was still pouring out of it.

'I'm OK,' I said. 'Get this,' and I picked up the hose, and sprayed Robbie all over his head. Then he shot some more at me with his gun, and Julie grabbed it and sprayed Greg, and Greg snatched the hose out of my hands and soaked Julie some more, and I got the gun off Julie and blasted Robbie.

You know what it's like when you get wet. Really wet, I mean. First it's your arms and legs and head. Then water trickles down your back and front. You get wetter and wetter. And wetter. Then you realise that there's not one dry bit on you. You couldn't get any wetter if you tried.

That's what it was like, for Robbie and Greg and Julie and me. Julie found an old bucket under a bush and filled it up with water. Robbie went on shooting with his water gun. Greg ran indoors and found a couple of sponges. He kept wetting them and throwing them at us.

We were laughing now too. We were screaming with laughter. Shrieking. Our sides hurt, our eyes were streaming and we could hardly stand up any more. We were covered in mud from head to foot.

We must have made a terrible noise. Windows were going up all along the row of houses.

'Julie!' someone was calling from Julie's side. 'What are you doing? Come back here at once!'

'Robbie! Greg!' someone was calling from the other side. 'Stop all that noise!'

We stopped and looked each other up and down.

'She's going to kill me,' said Julie.

'She's going to murder us,' said Greg.

'I'm a dead man,' I said.

There was a long silence. I could see in their faces that they were remembering how we'd started off. It could all go wrong again. Badly wrong.

I swallowed.

'Why don't we go into the base – I mean your base – till they've all cooled off a bit,' I said, watching their faces.

Robbie and Greg glanced at each other.

'Could do,' said Robbie.

He threw down his water pistol and pushed past me. I could see he wanted to go in first. I let him. I needed to talk to Julie.

'I didn't mean that about the pig.' I said. 'It was just – you were hot, right? You were a bit pink and that.'

She frowned. I could see she was still a bit offended.

'I can't help going pink. My mum says I've got sensitive skin.'

'Yeah, well, I'm sorry, anyway.'

She was doing something funny to her hair, fluffing it over her eyes and pushing out her mouth to make her face look longer.

'So what do you think? Do I look like a dog now, or what?'

That's the trouble with girls. You never know what you're supposed to say. I was about to go, 'No, of course you don't', but the truth was, she did look like a dog. Like one of those poodles with a fancy hair cut.

'Well . . . '

She saw I was embarrassed and laughed.

'You're allowed to say yes. I want to look like a dog. I'm desperate to have a dog. Mum says maybe next year.'

'OK, then. You do look like a dog. Brilliant, in fact.'

'Are you coming in here, or what?' Robbie called out from inside the base.

It was a bit awkward, to be honest, going in there. It felt like their space. And I was ashamed that I'd been so angry before. But then Mum called out again, and this time I could tell that she really, really meant it.

'James, if you don't come back here at once, I'll get the men to take your computer away and dump it.'

'I've got to go,' I said.

'What sort of computer is that then?' asked Greg.

I told him.

They looked at each other again.

'I suppose this is your base now really, being in your garden,' said Robbie.

'My garden?'

I looked round, seeing it properly for the first time. We hadn't had a garden at the old place. I hadn't known that having one would be good.

'Needs a bit of work, doesn't it?' I said. 'Bit of a roof to keep out the rain? I'll see if there's anything left over from the move. And there'll need to be another chair in here now too.'

'James!' shrieked Mum

'She means it,' I said. 'Got to go. See you later.'

'Yeah, see you,' they said.

RED-HANDED

KEITH GRAY

We were marched into the Head's office, lined up in front of his desk and warned not to move a muscle, not to make a sound. Matty Mitchell, Gary Bowers and me. We weren't friends, we were suspects.

When the Head burst in he looked like a muzzled crocodile – desperate to bite. He glared at us over the top of his glasses. 'Disgusting,' he told us. 'I'm *appalled*. Do you *hear* me?'

We fidgeted, looked at our feet.

I wasn't sure if he'd only been told about the graffiti, or had actually gone to the castle to see it with his own eyes. Sprayed in bright red paint at the bottom of the Lang Steps, and on the outside wall of St Margaret's Chapel, and even along the fat barrel of Mons Meg, were the worst swear words imaginable. In huge letters. Someone had covered Edinburgh Castle in the kind of language that would make your grandmother shrivel.

The Head shook with rage. It was a cramped office anyway, but his anger made it feel even smaller. When he bellowed it felt like his voice might burst the walls open. 'The thought that one of the pupils at my school would do such a thing is simply *appalling*.' He paced up and down behind his desk, so angry he couldn't stand still. 'It is a privilege to wear this school's uniform. This school is well respected in Edinburgh for its traditions, almost as much as the castle itself. Whichever one of you committed this disgusting crime is going to regret each and every letter he sprayed. Because that pupil is a *disgrace* to the uniform he's wearing.' He stared at us, glared at us. 'Smarten yourselves up.'

I pushed the knot of my tie higher and with my finger-tips very carefully straightened my blazer lapels. Bowers just tried to look like his blazer was able to fit his bulk. And Matty stood dithering. He already looked about as spick and span, neat and tidy as anyone could get – as though his mother had ironed his uniform only moments ago. But it was obvious from his tearful face that he'd never been called up in front of the Head before. Although it was nothing surprising for Bowers to be here – he probably kept a fold-down bed and slippers in the cupboard. I'd been here only once before. Yesterday. And I'd been standing next to Bowers that time too.

'I want this matter resolved quickly, understand?' The Head scowled at us in turn. His narrow eyes searched our faces one at a time for the tiniest hint of guilt. 'You were each seen skulking away from the rest of your class at least once during your visit to the castle this morning. I have witnesses. So I *know* it was one of you. If you are honest enough to own up here, now, then perhaps I could see a way of being more lenient in your punishment.'

He waited, watching us to see if his words were sinking in. But we knew it was the biggest lie and oldest trick in the Teachers' Handbook. We kept quiet.

'No one?' the Head asked, a single eyebrow raised. 'No one is going to be mature enough to admit to this crime? The disgusting vandal must also be a *coward*. And you force me to weed him out? So be it.'

He walked around from behind his desk. The three of

us took a wary step backwards. He stood in front of Bowers and held out his hand.

'Your locker key.'

Bowers's thick brows creased in confusion. 'What?'

'Don't *what* me, boy. Give me your locker key. You and I will search your locker – and woe betide if I discover a can of red spray-paint inside.'

'It wasn't me,' Bowers said. 'Why pick on me? Why not search their lockers?'

Mr Rodd narrowed his eyes at me and Matty. 'Don't you worry, Mr Bowers. You can be sure I'll be searching *everybody's* locker.'

He ushered Bowers through the door, but not before ordering Matty and I to stay exactly where we were and not so much as squeak, threatening us with his secretary who was sitting right outside. Matty was so nervous he couldn't stand still. He fiddled with his tie, tugged at the sleeves of his blazer, whined like a long-tailed cat in a roomful of rocking chairs.

'If you didn't do it, you've got nothing to worry about,' I whispered.

'Of course I didn't do it,' Matty hissed. 'You don't think I'd do something like that, do you?'

I shrugged. 'I'm just saying—'

'It was Bowers,' he said. 'It had to be. He's always in trouble. Look at what he did to you.'

I couldn't look at what he'd done to me because what he 'did' was my face. I had a nasty cut on the bridge of my nose, black and yellow bruising under my eyes and pain like you wouldn't believe, every time I sneezed. Although it hurt even more to think that Bowers didn't have a single mark on him. He'd fought dirty, grabbing me by my lapels and head-butting me hard enough to knock me on my backside. It had been a quick fight, but it was also how come I'd ended up standing in this office with him yesterday. I was desperate for revenge, but knew I'd never beat him with my fists.

When Bowers and the Head returned to the office, Bowers was looking all smug and cocky. As far as he was concerned, he was in the clear. This time it was Matty's locker key the Head wanted.

'It wasn't me, Sir,' Matty said. 'I had a poorly stomach. I had to go to the toilet, Sir. That's why I left the rest of the class. Because of my poorly stomach, Sir.'

Bowers sniggered as Matty was led away, said, 'See you later, Math-spew.' Which won him another threat from the Head. Not that he cared.

'You know what I reckon?' he asked me, once we were alone in the stuffy office. 'I reckon it was you, Johnny. I mean, Matty probably doesn't even understand what those words mean anyway. So I reckon it was your sick mind that came up with them.'

'Yeah, couldn't be you,' I said. 'You wouldn't have been able to get all the spelling right, even if it is the kind of thing you usually write in your mum's birthday cards.'

He sneered at me, scrunching up his already ugly face. 'You could've warped my brain with your disgusting language. I should sue you for it. I hope you get kicked out of school.'

I sighed, bored. 'Shut up, Bowers.'

'Gonna make me? Like you did yesterday?'

I knew he was staring at my swollen nose and the heavy bruises under my eyes. Looking at them like an artist looks at a painting he's proud of.

'You were lucky. I won't fall for the same trick twice.' I pointed at my blazer's lapels, daring him to grab hold exactly the way he'd done yesterday.

He just laughed at me.

'Come on,' I said. 'See what happens this time.'

He kept laughing until Matty and the Head returned. Matty looked flushed with relief.

'Right.' The Head clenched his jaw. 'Your locker key, John.' He beckoned for me to follow him.

'It must be him, Sir,' Bowers piped up. 'You've searched our lockers. It's disgusting what he's done, Sir. Just like you said. Appalling and—'

'Silence, Bowers. And *stay* silent until I return.'

I was pleased the Head had at last managed to shut Bowers up, but was reluctant to follow him. I stayed two or three steps behind all the way along the corridor to my locker. Because the problem was: Bowers was right. I was the vandal.

I'd sneaked away from our class when I'd thought the

teacher wasn't looking. I'd dodged the tourists and sprayed Mons Meg, St Margaret's Chapel, then I'd run down the Lang Steps and done them too. But I was determined not to take the blame.

*

Of course, there was no empty can of red spray-paint inside my locker. I'm not that daft. The Head clicked his tongue in sharp annoyance when he saw that the only contents were half a packet of Polos and my French text book. I was lucky he didn't lift the book up to peek underneath because then he would have seen the careless smeared red thumb-print, which would have given me away in a second.

'So . . . ' the Head said, his face darkening, his eyes bulging even more behind his glasses. 'I see. So . . . ' He snorted a hot, bullish breath through his nose. 'Right. Follow me.' He slammed my locker door closed and ordered me back along the corridor the way we'd come.

I enjoyed the look on Bowers' face when the Head and I returned to the office. He'd been imagining all sorts of humiliating punishments for me to suffer and couldn't hide his disappointment when he learned my locker had been empty of spray cans too. We were old enemies, but yesterday was the first time we'd fought. And, believe it or not, that made me lucky. He was a bully and a thug, and old enemies with most of the other kids too – hassling them any chance he got. It was about time somebody stood up to him. His day of reckoning was long overdue.

The Head paced back and forth behind his desk. 'Don't presume for one moment that I won't get to the bottom of this,' he said. 'You are the *only* pupils who were known to have gone missing from the tour group this morning, and if no *individual* is willing to take responsibility, then my only option is to believe you *all* had a hand in the crime.'

The three of us started talking at once. Matty went on about his 'poorly stomach'. Bowers reckoned he'd accidentally got lost. And I said I'd been to the gift shop to buy something for my mum. I even had a box of tablet to prove it. (It was just that I'd bought it last night from a shop on Princes Street.)

'Quiet!' The Head shouted. He paced back and forth again, but never took his eyes off us. 'I hope the three of you realise this is a criminal matter. I asked the police to let me deal with the offender in my own way, to which they agreed. But now I'm thinking perhaps I should contact them again. Perhaps I should have let them deal with the vandal themselves all along.'

That set off all our excuses again, the three of us desperate to out-shout each other.

The Head slammed his hand down onto his desk, ruffling his papers and rattling his pens, silencing us. 'I am going to leave the room for five minutes – no longer – while I decide how best to proceed in this matter. When

I return the vandal will be given one *final* opportunity to reveal himself. If that boy doesn't step forward, how-ever, I will be left with no alternative but to punish *all three of you.*'

I couldn't help feeling a niggling admiration for the Head as he left us alone. He was cleverer than he looked. He couldn't weed out the wrong-doer himself, so was forcing us to do it for him. He knew there was no honour among schoolboys backed into a corner.

As soon as the door closed, Bowers was in my face. 'Own up, Johnny. This isn't my fault. I'm not getting done because of you.'

I made sure I didn't flinch, no matter how bad his breath. 'Maybe Matty did it,' I said. 'He's the brainy one after all. Maybe that's why it's all spelt right.'

Matty looked like he might faint at the suggestion.

Bowers jabbed me in the shoulder. 'You think you're funny, don't you? But, see? I'm not laughing.' He shoved me hard. 'Own up or you'll wish I really had killed you yesterday.'

I wanted him all riled up. I wanted him angry enough to attack me. But I wanted him grabbing, not shoving. I turned to Matty. 'Why'd you do it? You seem like such a nice boy.'

Matty flapped his mouth like a dying fish.

Bowers jumped me from behind. 'It was you. Own up or die.' He forced me to the floor, punching me.

I managed to turn my face away at the last second as I

went down, saved my nose, but carpet-burned my cheek. I fought back, bucked him off and managed to scramble to my feet. I was in his face now.

'Come on then! Try it again. You won't get me twice!' And I pulled out the front of my blazer, taunting him, offering him my lapels so he could try to butt me like he had before. 'Come on!'

Unfortunately, I was all talk. He did get me twice. He grabbed my lapels. I couldn't have stopped him even if I'd wanted to. And he yanked me towards him while at the same time slamming his wide, solid forehead into my face.

I yelled out. My nose was a hot volcano of blood and hurt. I sagged in Bowers' grip. He held me up by my lapels for a second or two while he called me every name he could think of, then let me drop to the floor.

The Head charged into the room, bashing the door back on its hinges in his haste. He'd no doubt had an ear to the door and come running at Bowers's roar and my yell. 'Good God! What on earth . . . !'

'He did it,' I said from the floor. 'Bowers did it.'

The Head was aghast. 'I can see what he—'

'He's the vandal,' I said, struggling to my knees and then my feet. 'He sprayed the stuff at the castle.'

Bowers tried to protest. He held his hands up in innocence.

And that was when the Head saw the red spray-paint all over his fingers.

It was also when Bowers saw it for the first time too. He stared at his fingertips. 'But . . . it's not . . . I don't know how . . . '

I was dizzy. I had to lean against the wall. The blood from my broken nose gushed down my face, chin and neck, and covered the front of my blazer. Even with my lapels torn and rumpled where Bowers had grabbed them, no one could tell what was genuine blood and what was the red paint I'd sprayed behind them earlier.

'You get to the nurse,' the Head ordered me. 'Matthew, you take him. But you, you stay right here, Mr Bowers.'

Bowers still hadn't quite caught up with what was

happening. He couldn't take his eyes off his paint-smeared fingers. 'But . . . I . . . '

The Head banged his office door behind us as Matty led me out. Even from halfway along the corridor we could still hear him bellowing at Bowers.

'I knew he'd done it,' Matty said, his relief spilling over. 'I told you he had. I said so, didn't I?'

I straightened my blazer, dabbed at my nose and nodded in agreement. 'Yeah,' I said. 'Caught red-handed. No arguing with that.'

The Music Shop   JOHN FARDELL

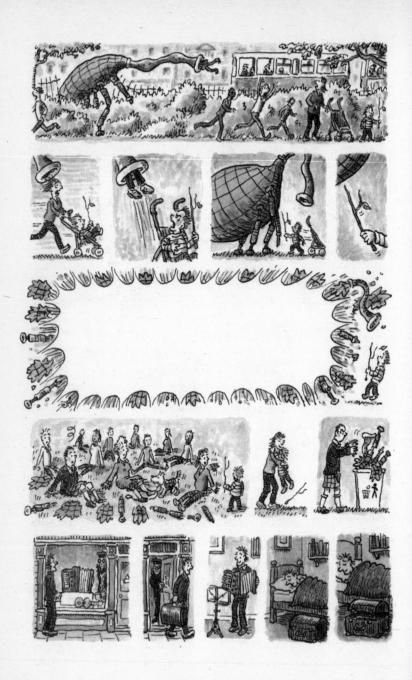

Word of Crow

VIVIAN FRENCH

'Hail, dark sister!' The voice was deep, and laden with doom.

'Hail to you, sister of the night!' The second voice was equally gloomy.

'Hail, hail, hail to us all three!' The third was deepest of all, suggesting death and destruction in equal proportions.

'Unless it rains instead, which it's more than likely to,

given the lie of the clouds,' said a fourth, and the three witches on top of the castle battlements swung round to stare.

'And who exactly do you think you are, interrupting a private meeting?' The tallest witch frowned at the very young and attractive witch hovering on her broomstick just below. 'I don't remember inviting you.'

The young witch settled herself on the edge of the wall. 'You didn't. But I heard it was your hailing night, so I thought I'd pop up to keep you company – oops! Watch it! Here comes the sentry!'

There was a swift flurry of black skirts and feathers, and four hooded crows were perching on the stones.

The sentry didn't give them a second glance as he passed, even though one was wearing a rusty old bonnet, and another had shiny black button-up boots. As soon as he was gone there was another flurry, and the witches returned to normal.

'You've got that down to a fine art,' the young witch said approvingly. 'Mother said you were experts.' Seeing a blank expression float across all three faces, she stood up and gave a little curtsey. 'I'm sorry. I thought you knew. I'm Moona Gristle . . . Mother Gristle's oldest. And I must say, I do like your hailing technique.' She nodded at the tallest witch. 'That death and destruction thing is truly wonderful, Mother Morgue.'

'Are you suggesting mine isn't?' The witch with the bonnet sounded offended. 'I was much admired at last year's Blackford Hill Cauldron Fest.'

Moona hastened to repair her mistake. 'No, no, Mother Venom . . . you sounded very scary. And as for Mother Dismal – heavens above!' She lifted her hands in admiration. 'What can I say?'

Mother Dismal gave her a suspicious glance, but said nothing.

'So to what, exactly, do we owe the honour of this visit?' Mother Morgue enquired.

'Well . . . ' Moona sat down again. 'I've sort of brought a message from Mother.' This was not strictly true, but Moona felt it was in the interests of her new and exciting job to stretch the truth a little. Or even a lot. 'Did you know that the Wise One on Salisbury Crags is looking for an assistant?' She hesitated, then added, 'All expenses paid. Food and lodging provided. Ability to fly unseen essential.'

There was a long and significant pause. Each of the

other three witches was well aware of this fact. Edinburgh was a small place, and Word of Crow and Cry of Cat never failed to spread any news at a remarkable speed amongst the witches, warlocks, magicians and sorcerers who lived or lurked in and around the city. Word of Crow had been particularly noisy recently; several of the elderly warlocks and magicians had put in a formal complaint. Their peaceful retirement, they wrote, was being severely interrupted. The sorcerers were mostly deaf, so hadn't noticed.

Mother Dismal was the first to break the silence. 'Actually,' she said carefully, 'I had heard something to that effect. '

'Me too,' said Mother Venom. 'As it happens. Can't remember who it was who told me, though. And of course, I couldn't be more interested . . . I mean LESS interested.' She began to look flustered. 'I mean, working for a Wise One? La di da! The very idea!'

Mother Morgue gave her colleagues a piercing look. 'How long have you known?' she asked sharply, and then added, 'my dear friends.' Her tone suggested that friends they were not, unless their replies were extremely satisfactory.

Moona saved the two witches from answering. 'So you DO know!' She clapped her hands and beamed. 'That's wonderful! So are you thinking of applying?' She put her head on one side, and gave a girlish giggle. 'What fun. He's asking anyone who's interested to come and see him tomorrow after sunset. Mother says he does an awful lot of good works, but then I'm quite sure you do too . . . from time to time.'

Again there was a silence. It was very clear that Moona was not going to get any further response, and she picked up her broomstick. 'I'd better be off. Lots of love, and I'll leave you to talk among yourselves. See you soon!' And she soared up into the midnight sky.

The silence continued, until Mother Dismal sighed. 'All right, then,' she said. 'I'm sorry. I should have said something before . . . but I thought it would sound foolish. Thinking of settling down to a job at my time of life.'

Mother Morgue gave a short embarrassed cough. 'Erm. I'm sorry too. And I don't see why we shouldn't think of working for someone else. Things aren't what they used to be, are they?'

'They certainly aren't.' Mother Venom shook her head. 'Personally, I blame the plague. I actually feel bad when I put a boil on someone's nose these days. They rush about screaming and shouting that the plague's come back, and everyone flaps and fusses, and then when it dies down and nobody's dead they start muttering about witchcraft. The next thing you know some poor old woman without an ounce of magic is being pointed at and then—'

'Stop!' Mother Morgue grabbed at Mother Venom's arm. 'Don't even mention it!' She shuddered. 'We all know what you mean.'

'And when was the last time any of us was asked for a charm? Or a curse?' Mother Dismal stared at her boots. 'When was the last time you were given a nice fat chicken or a sweet apple pie in exchange for a potion?'

'There's one big problem as I see it,' Mother Venom pointed out. 'That little minx was right. He's addicted to Good Deeds.'

Mother Dismal nodded. 'He might think we're unsuitable. I know we're not the worst of witches, but we can't exactly claim to be good.'

'Come, come.' Mother Venom smoothed her tattered black skirts. 'Who else is there for him to choose from? "Ability to fly unseen essential"? Mother Gristle uses a broomstick, and so does Mother Mincing.'

Mother Morgue, who had been looking thoughtful ever since Moona left, suddenly sat up straight. 'Ladies!' she said. 'I have an idea!'

Mother Dismal and Mother Venom looked hopeful, if wary. Mother Morgue's ideas were sometimes overly biased towards her own well-being.

'We will all three apply for the post!' The tall witch leapt to her feet. 'And tomorrow at daybreak we will take to the skies.'

'But if it's daybreak, we'll be seen,' Mother Venom objected.

Mother Morgue frowned. 'We'll be crows. Please don't interrupt.'

Mother Venom mumbled an apology, and subsided.

'We'll take to the skies, and search high and low . . . and we will do Good Deeds! We will do good from daybreak until sunset, and then . . . '

'And then?' Mother Dismal prompted.

'And then the Wise One can choose between us!'

Mother Venom and Mother Dismal looked at each other, then nodded.

'Agreed,' they said, and shook hands.

Moona Gristle was chuckling as she flew steadily over the Lawnmarket, down the High Street and over Netherbow Port. The air was fresher once she reached the large houses and gardens of Canongate, and she breathed in deeply as she sped down Abbey Strand. By the time she reached Salisbury Crags she had left behind the hideous smells of rotting food, dung, the contents of chamber pots and other human waste. She landed smoothly on top of the crags, and went to report to the Wise One.

Master Placidus was sitting admiring the stars, his back against a rock. His thoughts were of the city, and the people; much battered by endless wars with the English and plague and disease, he felt they could do with help. He thought of the steep slippery slopes of Fishmarket

Close, and shuddered. Tiny children, barefoot and dressed in rags, trying to sell cods' heads covered in mould in order to buy a crust of bread. Older children dodging in and out, filching anything they could lay their hands on. Women screaming and yelling as they saw their precious fish snatched away – fish that, if sold, might buy thin polluted milk for their snivelling skinny babies. But there were moments of true kindness. He had seen many a half starved old woman handing a young mother a hard earned penny, or a lad helping a well-dressed but doddery gentleman up the steps of one of the tall stone houses. If only, he thought, if only there could be a little more kindness. And fun . . .

This reminded him of Moona, and he glanced up at the moon to check the time. She should be back any minute, he thought, and smiled. When his old friend, Mother Gristle, had asked him to give the girl a week's work experience it had never occurred to him that he'd end up offering her a job. He was used to being on his own, but Moona's enthusiasm had been most refreshing. Her plan for persuading the witches to do Good Deeds was nothing short of sheer genius. He had wondered many times about asking them for help but, as Moona had been quick to point out when he mentioned it, that would almost undoubtedly have led to a flat refusal. This way it would seem to be all their own idea, which was always far more satisfactory. And Moona had done the organising as well. He stroked his chin, and smiled again. He was a modest man, and would never have thought that the possibility of being his assistant would send three senior witches into a sudden flurry of help-fulness and charity. The one glaring fault in the plan had been dismissed by Moona as no problem at all.

'But I don't actually want another assistant,' he had told her.

'Oh, don't worry about that.' She had sounded amazingly breezy. 'Just tell them the position's filled. But there might be another in a few months time . . . so it'll be worth their while to keep on with the charity work.'

The enchanter looked round. He was sure he had heard the sound of a broomstick landing, and he jumped to his feet as Moona came skipping towards him.

'Brilliant!' she said happily. 'I knew sending that message last week by Word of Crow would do the trick, even though I did get a sore throat. They'd all heard the news, and they were jumpy as cats when I mentioned it. I did a lower circle of the castle after I'd left them, and I heard them talking – and they were totally taken in.' She slung her broomstick behind a rock, and sat down. 'I did worry I might have gone a bit too far, actually, but it was OK. They're going to spend from sunrise to sundown tomorrow doing Good Deeds, and then they'll come and see you. And then you can say which of them has done the best, tell them the job's gone, and send them home.'

Master Placidus nodded, but was conscious of a small

71

nagging worry. The phrase 'false pretences' floated into his head. Did the end justify the means? It wasn't a question he'd ever had to answer before, and for the first time he wondered if the plan was such a good idea after all. But then again, he needed the help . . . and so did Edinburgh.

Master Placidus sighed, and decided to go to bed and sleep on it.

All three witches had a terrible night. They were not used to sleeping before the moon went down and getting up at dawn, and there was a distinct grumpiness in the air as they met once more on the castle battlements.

'Ark,' Mother Dismal croaked as she perched on the barrel of a large cannon. 'So where are we going to begin?'

'I've been thinking about it,' Mother Morgue announced, 'and I think we should each take a separate area.'

Mother Venom suppressed a yawn. 'Well, I'd like to work in the Grassmarket.'

Mother Morgue gave her a quick sideways glance. 'No pecking at dead men's eyes, I hope.'

'Really!' Mother Venom sounded genuinely affronted. 'I thought we were supposed to be doing good? Besides, there aren't any hangings today.'

'I'd like Fishmarket Close.' Mother Dismal straightened a feather.

'And I'll take the High Street.' Mother Morgue nodded. 'Especially round the Tolbooth and the Mercat Cross.' She saw the expression on Mother Dismal's face. 'I'll be very careful. I won't touch your area. Anyway, you can always go down into Cowgate. There's plenty goes on down there.'

A ray of sun pierced the heavy clouds, and touched the top of the castle. At once the three crows rose up into the air, and headed towards the city below.

The day started well enough. Mother Dismal stole a large mackerel from one of the more well-to-do fish booths and dropped it at the feet of a grubby urchin who was crying in the gutter. Mother Venom flapped under the nose of a horse that was in danger of hauling a cartload of cabbages over a drunken huckster lying in the street. Mother Morgue squawked loudly as a sly-looking woman was about to slip her hand into the market basket of an anxious little servant girl. Glowing with virtue, the three crows met on top of the Mercat Cross to gloat and catch their breath.

'How easy was that?' Mother Morgue enquired, with a flick of her tail.

Mother Venom nodded. 'No trouble at all.'

Mother Dismal looked smug. 'My wee boy's smiling fit to burst!'

But when the three crows returned to check the progress of their good deeds, all was not well. The urchin was now facing an irate fishmonger, who was demanding to know how he had come by such a fine fish. The driver of the cart of cabbages had jumped down and was manhandling the drunk out of the road by his heels, bumping his head at every step. The sly woman had elbowed the servant girl as she hurried away, and upset her purchases into a deeply unpleasant heap of old and rotting vegetables. A pig eyed a bunch of red ribbons thoughtfully, then ate them.

'It's much harder than I thought,' Mother Dismal complained, as she and Mother Morgue passed on the wing.

'You must have tried to help the wrong person,' was the cross response as Mother Morgue flew up to a chimney pot to observe the crowds below. As she landed, she noticed another much younger crow on a neighbouring pot. It looked familiar, and was studying her with interest, but when she raised a wing in greeting it flew swiftly away.

The day went on with varying degrees of success. A flower seller lost three of his finest blooms as Mother Venom attempted to make the bumpy course of love run a little smoother, and he was still shaking his fist when

he was rewarded with a silk handkerchief from a lawyer's pocket. The lawyer was not compensated. Mother Venom had seen him step over a tiny child begging for a penny. Mother Dismal carried a large crust to a small girl looking after her even smaller sister; the owner of the crust chased her down the close, but when he saw the girls he stopped, shrugged, and went away. Mother Morgue was flying in and out of the many booths squashed between St Giles and the Tolbooth, quite unaware she was being watched.

A pleasant looking young man was leaning out of a window; as he saw Mother Morgue swoop on a dropped coin and carry it triumphantly to a beggar sitting in a dark corner, his eyebrows rose and he leaned out further, knocking a sheet of paper off the table at his side. The paper sailed out, but before it could touch the ground a boy leaped up and caught it. He stood still to read the words, and began to smile. A friend tapped him on the shoulder and asked what he was reading, and when the boy showed him, he smiled too. Mother Morgue was seized with an idea.

When the boys let the paper fall she swooped to catch it, and dropped it at the beggar's feet. He, however, shook his head; it was a young woman who picked it up and read it, and she laughed out loud. She tucked it into her pocket; it was with some difficulty that Mother Morgue removed it to pass on to a group of swaggering lads.

'H'm,' they said, 'it's a poem,' and they too read and laughed, then folded the paper into a dart and tossed it in the air.

Mother Morgue retrieved the poem once more but, deciding it was looking rather the worse for wear, flew up to the window to return it to its owner.

By the end of the day the three crows were exhausted. They gathered together to straighten their feathers, then flew wearily towards Salisbury Crags. Landing behind a convenient rock, they shook themselves back into old women, arranged their long black dresses, and rested for a moment.

'So how did you do?' Mother Dismal asked.

Mother Venom sighed. She had fully intended to boast, but she kept remembering the carter hauling the drunk across the cobbles, and was uncomfortably aware that it might have been her fault. Mother Dismal was equally depressed, imagining her street urchin carried off to the Tolbooth. Mother Morgue, made of sterner stuff, was concentrating on her successes and resolutely ignoring the memory of the little servant girl's expression when she saw her ribbons vanish. Nevertheless, she appeared to be in no hurry to present herself in front of the Wise One, and the three witches sat on into the gathering twilight.

'Maybe we should leave it for another day,' Mother Venom said at last.

'We might get better with practice,' Mother Dismal agreed.

Mother Morgue considered. 'True . . . but Master Placidus expects us tonight.' She stood up and dusted her skirts. 'Are you coming?'

Mother Dismal stayed sitting where she was. 'I've just thought of something,' she said.

'Which is?' Mother Morgue sat down again.

'If Master Placidus offers one of us the job, what happens to the other two?'

Mother Venom nodded. 'I was wondering about that. I mean, you can't have a hailing unless there's three of you. Nor a cauldron fest. Nor—'

Mother Morgue swung round, her eyes flashing. 'You mean we've spent all day working as we've never worked before, and all for nothing?'

There was a pause, then Mother Dismal said, 'I suppose I am . . . but don't you think it was rather satisfactory when things went well?'

'I know a cold-hearted lawyer who's going to miss his fine silk handkerchief,' Mother Venom gloated, then added, 'I might go down to the Grassmarket again tomorrow. Not for all day, mind. Just for an hour or two . . . as a crow, of course.'

Most unexpectedly, Mother Morgue began to laugh. Her friends stared at her in astonishment as her shoulders shook and tears ran down her cheeks.

'What is it?' Mother Venom asked anxiously.

'I just realised something.' Mother Morgue blew her nose, and wiped her eyes. 'I saw this little crow watching me, and I knew I recognised it, but I couldn't think where from. And I've just remembered. It was Moona Gristle – the girl who came to see us last night. And you know what? I remembered something else. Mother Gristle's been away for at least a week, so there's no way she'd have sent us a message. We've been set up, ladies. Set up by that girl.' Mother Morgue blew her nose again, and her face changed. '"The Wise One on Salisbury Crags wants an assistant"!' The old witch was sneering now. 'Well, do you know what I think? I think clever little Moona's hiding somewhere just waiting for us to make fools of ourselves . . . but she's not going to make a fool out of me!' Mother Morgue stamped her foot. 'I'm going home, right this minute!'

'Mother Morgue! One moment, if you please.' The Wise One's voice was soft, but it brought with it a curious stillness. 'Please don't be angry . . . you have done so well today.' He moved forward from the shadows, and settled himself on a large boulder. 'All three of you . . . you have all done well.'

'But we were tricked into it, weren't we?' Mother Morgue still sounded angry.

Master Placidus bowed his head. 'I misjudged you,' he said. 'I thought if I asked you to undertake good and charitable deeds you would refuse.'

Mother Morgue snorted. 'You're quite right.'

There was a rustle of skirts, and Moona Gristle appeared carrying a tray of glasses filled with a liquid that shone and sparkled. Mother Morgue bristled.

'H'mph,' she said. 'It's you.' She gave Moona a long hard stare. 'But do you know what? Not many girls your age could fool me. Although,' she added with some satisfaction, 'I did find you out in the end.'

Moona grinned. 'So you did. Shall we drink to your success?'

'Indeed we should,' said Master Placidus.

'Noooo!' There was a loud wail from Mother Dismal, and she shook her head. 'I wasn't a success. I'm sorry, but I can't stop thinking about it. There's a child accused of stealing, and it's all my fault.'

Moona looked at her. 'Oh no,' she said. 'I thought you'd seen. The woman on the crab stall spoke up for him. And the fishmonger needed  a boy to run errands, so now young Wilfie has a job.' She turned to Mother Venom. 'Perhaps you don't know, either. Your carter went back to see what he'd done, and he and

79

his victim spent the afternoon in the White Horse toasting each other.'

'Tell Mother Morgue what she did,' the Wise One prompted.

'You gave the poet

the idea of opening a library, so instead of catching words in the street, books can be borrowed, and read again and again.'

'H'mph.' Mother Morgue was pleased, but did not intend to show it. 'What about the red ribbons?'

'Gone,' Moona told her, and winked. 'But the owner of the pig was a quite exceptionally handsome boy . . . '

Mother Dismal sighed happily. 'That's SO lovely. What a nice ending to the day.'

The Wise One leaned back, delighted that peace and harmony had been restored. He raised his glass. 'May I propose a toast?'

'You may not.' Mother Morgue stood up. 'We have to get home. We have things to do tomorrow.' She gave Moona a hard stare. 'And we can manage quite well on our own, thank you, Miss. We're quite capable of keeping an eye on things ourselves. If you want something to do, you'd better take this non-existent post of assistant yourself. It might stop you interfering—' She stopped. 'Of course! You ARE the assistant, aren't you?'

Moona shook her head, and Master Placidus sat up, startled. Moona patted his shoulder. 'I'm sorry,' she said. 'I'm going to resign. I'm going to work with Mother Dismal, Mother Venom and Mother Morgue . . . '

Mother Morgue pursed her lips. 'I don't remember asking you.'

'You didn't. I'm asking myself. I think you're wonderful.'

'H'mph,' Mother Morgue remarked, but said nothing more. As the four crows rose into the starlit night the Wise One waved, and went back to his cave. As he sat down, he sighed wistfully.

'A wonderful woman indeed,' he said, then hiccupped, and went to sleep.

81

The Storyteller

ALISON FLETT

Hey! Listen tae this. I'm gonnae tell you a secret, something that naebody else kens. I dinnae ken why but I feel like I can trust you. It feels like you might be someone a bit like me, someone whae likes stories, someone whae kens that words can be magic. So here it is; ma secret. I'm gonnae write it sideways in case somebody else is reading this ower your shoulder. I'm no wanting just anybody tae see it:

This story isnae really meant tae be here. It got intae the book by magic.

Pretty mental, ay? Anyway I'm glad I've telt you cos now I can tell you all the other stuff too, all aboot the crazy things I seen in the secret room under the ground. It's good sometimes, being able tae tell somebody things. In ma hoose you cannae tell anybody ANYTHING. If I telt ma big sister Jade this story she would laugh her heid off and call me a nutter.

I could tell ma ma but she would likely be doing something else and she would just go, 'is that right, Jenny? That's nice hen', and I would ken she hadnae been listening.

Ma da's aboot the only one whae WOULD listen but ma da doesnae stay wi us any mair. He stays wi a wifie called Mary in one ae they new flats in Muirhouse Avenue, and if me or Jade see them in the street we're meant tae say NOTHING tae them. We're meant tae WALK PAST and IGNORE THEM. It's nae bother ignoring Mary cos I dinnae like her but it's dead hard tae ignore ma da, specially if he shouts oan me or tries tae speak tae me. I wish he would just come hame.

When ma da stayed at hame wi us things were different. Right enough, there were mair arguments, him and ma ma at it the WHOLE time, but at least I used tae speak then. When ma da left I stopped speaking. I dinnae ken why. It just got harder tae say things somehow, so it wis easier tae say nothing tae naebody. Ma ma got mad wi me tae begin wi. She said I wis being rude, no answering her. She said she wis gonnae keep me in, stop ma pocket money, she tried all sorts tae get me speaking. None ae it made any difference. Then she went and took me tae the doctor and the doctor telt her just tae gie it time and eventually I'd start speaking again. I thought 'aye right I will!' but I didnae say anything, obviously. At least it meant she stopped hassling me. Jade didnae but. Jade still gied me a poke every time she went past, trying tae get me tae shout at her. She still mumbled 'nutter' under her breath whenever I wis close enough tae hear.

It wisnae that I wis short ae words, mind you, I done plenty speaking tae masel. I telt stories in ma heid, ower and ower. Ma da used tae tell us stories. 'Goldilocks' and 'Sleeping Beauty', and sometimes ones he made up aboot me and Jade. After he left I started making up ma ain stories. I had a favourite one aboot Jade getting eaten by a crocodile, and another one where ma da took me away on a special holiday, just me and him. That's how the bairns fae the underground room found me; it wis because I wis telling masel stories.

It wis a right dreich Saturday, the day it happened. Ma wis at work and it wis raining so me and Jade were stuck in the flat. The whole place was a tip. It was like when ma da left, ma ma just totally stopped cleaning. There wis piles ae washing lying all over the sofa and chairs, dirty plates and an overflowing ashtray oan the coffee table, half empty cans ae beans and totally empty vodka bottles littering the worktops in the kitchen. The only place that wis vaguely tidy wis ma bedroom. I wis sitting in there looking oot the windae at the street doon below. The gang ae stray dogs that ran roond oor bit had got intae one ae the rubbish bags and there wis auld tins and plastic wrappers, newspaper pages and the stoor oot ae a hoover bag scattered all up oor path.

I picked up ma set ae Russian dolls that wis sitting oan the windae-sill. Ma da had bought them for me when I wis just a baby. There used tae be four dolls inside each other but one had got lost, the wee-est one. I pulled apart the three that wis left and fixed them thegither again, separately. I wis lining them all up oan the windae-sill when the bedroom door banged open. I turned roond. Jade wis standing there wi a cereal packet in her hand. 'Hey Jenny,' she went, 'did you eat all the Coco Pops again?'

I didnae say nothing.

She marched across the room and stuck the empty packet under ma nose. 'There wis LOADS left yesterday,' she said. 'You're nothing but a greedy wee FREAK!' She skelped me roond the side ae the heid wi the box so I jabbed ma elbow backwards intae her stomach. She grabbed a haud ae ma hair and wis pulling ma heid doon when we both deeked Da and Mary oot the windae, walking roond the corner fae Muirhouse Drive intae the Medway. Jade let go ma hair and we watched the pair ae them coming up the street towards oor flat. Mary had her arms roond ma da's waist and she wis saying something intae his ear. He turned tae look up at the flat as they went past so me and Jade both ducked doon beneath the windae.

We sat there thegither for a wee minute then Jade went, 'It's your fault he left anyway. If you werenae such a freak he wouldnae have wanted tae move in wi that cow.' She stood up, kicked me in the ankle and walked oot the room, leaving the cereal box and three Coco Pops lying oan the carpet.

I started tae greet. I kent it wisnae really true. I kent Jade had just said it cos she wis angry aboot him going away, but it still hurt.

I rubbed the wet off ae ma cheeks wi the back ae ma hand and sat doon oan the chair by the windae. It wis raining harder, the drops hammering oan the scattered cans, turning the newspaper tae a sodden slush. I started telling masel a story aboot the street flooding and Jade floating away oan her bed. I had just made her disappear intae the sea when I seen something ootside. The tears in ma eyes and the rain oan the windae were making everything blurry, so I didnae believe it at first. It looked like a couple ae bairns were waving tae me fae the other side ae the street. I wiped ma eyes again and leant forwards, peering through the glass. They were definitely there, a laddie and lassie aboot ma age wi the weirdest looking claes oan. They had sheepskin coats and big felt boots and tall furry hats. They were baith gawping up at me, waving like mad wi big grins oan their coupons. I stood looking doon at them, then I went and got oan ma shoes and ma waterproof jacket, opened the front door and went doon the stair.

Oor intercom wisnae working again so somebody had stopped the main door fae shutting by using a lump ae breeze block as a jamb. I pulled the door open and it crashed back against the stone behind me as I tugged up ma hood and stepped oot intae the teeming rain. The laddie and lassie were doon the bottom ae the street, waving at me tae follow. I ran after them, turning right along Muirhouse Drive, ma trainers slapping doon oan the wet paving slabs.

When I caught up wi them they baith stopped. The laddie looked at me. 'Hello,' he went. 'I'm Vanya.' He had a funny kind ae voice, like he wis fae somewhere else, no Scotland. He held oot his hand and I shook it. He gripped ma fingers dead tight and looked intae ma face, blue eyes all twinkly below his furry hat. 'Yes,' he says, 'you're a storyteller alright.' He turned tae the lassie. 'What do you reckon, Maroosia?'

87

The lassie walked taewards me and cupped her hands roond either side ae ma face. Raindrops fell oan her cheeks and dripped fae the end ae her nose as she looked straight intae ma eyes. 'Oh yes,' she said. 'Definitely.' She smiled at me. 'I knew anyway, when I saw you at the window,' she said. 'I could see the story leaking out of you, hanging in the air above your head. We thought you might like to meet our grandfather. Come on. Come with us.'

She took ma hand and led me along the path taewards the shopping centre. Some older laddies fae the school skidded past us oan skateboards, their wheels racketing oan the paving cracks, and as we got closer tae the shops I could see a gang ae mums wi bairns in buggies standing blethering ootside the bookies. It wis strange, everything else carrying oan as usual while this pair went oan aboot storytellers and grandfathers. I wis pretty sure they were either nutters or they'd got me mixed up wi someone else, but I went wi them anyway.

Just before we reached the shops they steered me intae the library. The doors closed behind us, shutting oot all the ootside noise, and we stood in the warm and the quiet, oor claes steaming a wee bit in the heat. It felt like a different world. Peaceful. A librarian wis standing behind the counter, sorting through a pile ae books. A few other folk walked up and doon looking at the books oan the shelves. Vanya and Maroosia took me ower tae the children's section. We stopped between two sets ae shelves, hidden fae the others in the library by the rows ae books.

'Listen,' Vanya went. 'Our grandfather is a great storyteller and if you come with us now he will give you one of his stories. If you're lucky, maybe he will also share some of his magic with you. What do you say? Will you come?'

I grinned at him and nodded. I wanted tae find oot mair aboot this grandad storyteller person.

Vanya hunkered doon on the flair and rolled back a strip ae carpet. There wis a wooden door underneath it. He grabbed the handle wi baith hands and hefted it open, falling backwards as it thudded doon oan the carpet. A battered wooden staircase led fae the doorway doon tae a basement room that flickered and glowed wi an  orange light. 'After you,' said Vanya, waving his hand at the hole.

I stood there for a wee minute, then I took a deep breath and made ma way doon the stairs. What I seen when I reached the bottom ae it wis awesome. I wis in this huge low-ceilinged room. All the walls were lined wi bookshelves, apart fae the one furthest away, where a load ae blazing logs sparked and danced in a fireplace, filling the room wi a warm glow. The books were kind ae shining too, blues and greens and reds and purples seeping oot fae between their pages, making rainbows that hung above the shelves. There wis giant tapestries hung oan either side ae the fireplace wi pictures woven intae them in threads ae gold and silver. When the firelight caught the pictures they seemed tae move across the tapestry all by theirselves. A thick forest ae trees sparkled wi frost, and above it this amazing winged ship wis sailing across the sky. A golden fish raised its heid fae the waters ae a rippling silver river, and a weird wee hut wi chicken legs strode along the riverbank taewards the forest.

The low ceiling wis held up by rows ae wooden pillars, all painted tae look like trees, wi deer keeking roond the trunks and owls and squirrels hiding in the branches. The bare wooden floor wis covered wi thick soft rugs made fae sheepskin and dark broon fur. By the fire sat an auld man in a battered armchair, a wee wooden table by his side. His breeks were tucked intae the same kind ae boots that the bairns had oan and he wis wearing a sheepskin waistcoat. A clay pipe wis gritted between his teeth and smoke pirled and spiralled fae it, making crazy patterns in the air.

'This is our grandfather,' said Maroosia. 'To most people he is known as Old Peter.'

90

The auld man took the pipe fae between his teeth and his bright blue eyes crinkled intae a warm smile. 'Hello, storyteller,' he said.

I looked doon at ma feet.

'Well,' he said, 'I can see you have your own stories inside you. Good. That is good. I need someone like you to share my magic with.' He bent forwards, knocked his pipe intae the fire and laid it doon oan the hearth. 'I wonder,' he said, settling back intae his chair and stroking his fingers through his long grey beard, 'would you like to hear a story of mine?' I nodded. 'Vanya, Maroosia, get me my things, little pigeons,' he said.

The children hurried tae the fireplace and heaved back the tapestries. There wis cupboard doors hidden behind the heavy material. They each opened one ae the doors and took something oot. Vanya brung a pile ae curled yellow parchment ower tae his grandfather, and Maroosia carried a huge golden feather and a bottle ae silver-coloured ink. They laid the stuff doon oan the wee table by his side.

'Thank you, little ones,' he said. 'Now, what colour of story shall we have today?'

'I want a red one,' said Vanya, birling aboot the room wi his arms flailing. 'An angry, devilish red one!'

Maroosia tilted her heid tae one side and stared intae the fire. 'I think a blue one,' she said, 'a wistful, melancholy blue.'

Their grandfather smiled and turned tae me. 'How

about you, little pigeon,' he said, and I felt ma heart leap and flutter when he called me that.

'Go on,' said Maroosia. 'You choose.'

I looked doon at ma feet again, the scuffed toes ae ma trainers, the frayed ends ae ma jeans. I pointed tae the dark green ae ma waterproof jacket and looked at Old Peter.

He nodded. 'A green one,' he said. 'A dark forest green. So it shall be.' He twirled open the lid ae the bottle and dipped the end ae the golden feather intae it. Different shades ae green rolled and rippled through the silvery ink, until the whole bottle wis the sparkling jade green ae a deep warm ocean that changed as I watched it tae the bright green ae grass waving in the sun, and then the pale yellowy green ae a Golden Delicious apple. The ink went oan shimmering and changing while the auld man held the feather above the parchment and began tae speak.

'Once upon a time,' he went, and the feather done a wee dance ower the page, spilling dark green words across it. As it moved fae left tae right, I seen the O ae 'Once' growing bigger all by itself, swelling up like a balloon and sprouting shoots that curled across the paper, framing the auld man's words wi leafy patterns. *There was a boy and a girl, who lived with their grandfather in a wooden hut at the edge of a great forest,'* Old Peter went on. I watched wi ma mooth open as a totsy green hut rose up fae the page. The tops ae dark green pine trees also poked through

the parchment, growing taller and taller till they towered ower the log hut, waving and rustling in a bit breeze that wis blowing across the table. The door ae the wee hut burst open and a teensy lassie and laddie tumbled oot ae it, bawling blue murder at each other.

'Look Vanya, it's us!' cried Maroosia, and right enough, the wee lassie and laddie looked dead like Vanya and Maroosia, same claes and everything.

'One day,' Old Peter went, *'the children were arguing most terribly, and their poor old grandfather grew tired of the noise. "My dears, you must go out to play," he said. "Go and find something to do together in the warm sun."*

The children did as their grandfather asked, for they were good little pigeons really, but once outside the girl stormed away from her brother in a fury, taking the path that led into the forest. After her went her brother, calling, "Maroosia, come back! You must not go in there for there are dangers in the darkness." Maroosia just snorted and tossed her long hair over her shoulders and carried on walking, with Vanya hurrying behind.

"Maroosia!" Vanya called again, "are you forgetting the witch with the iron teeth who lives in a hut with chicken legs? If she smells you she will send her hut running after you into the forest." Once more Maroosia only laughed, and strode onwards through the trees.

Deeper and deeper into the forest they went, and darker and darker it grew. The path dwindled away to nothing, and at last Maroosia stopped, realising she was lost. Vanya caught up with his sister and he shouted angrily, "Now look what you've done! We're lost and it's all your fault. We'll never be able to find our way home."

"It's not MY fault," Maroosia shouted back. "I didn't ask you to follow me. If you had left me alone, I wouldn't have come so far trying to get away from you." And so their argument started all over again, their shouts ringing loudly through the forest.

Suddenly, right in the middle of the shouting, they heard a high-pitched voice call out "Enough!" Maroosia and Vanya were so astonished that they stopped and looked all around them.

"Oh no," whispered Vanya, "it's the witch with the iron teeth!"

The tiny voice came again. "Witch, ha!" it shouted. "Does this look like a witch's face?"

"We don't know," said Maroosia. "We can't see you."

And the voice replied, "Because you are not looking in the right place."

Vanya and Maroosia looked down at their feet, and there,

standing next to a tree stump, was a tiny man, no bigger than one of their fingers. His skin was brown and shiny as a nut, and his clothes were brown too, so that he was almost invisible against the forest floor.

"Listen," he shouted up to them, "I can't stand this noise
                                                                           you make.
With the arguments in our village too, it's more than I can take."

Then he sat down on a tree root and put his head in his hands. His tiny shoulders shook as he began to cry.

Vanya and Maroosia looked at each other and then
they both lay flat on the
ground beside the little
man. Maroosia stretched
out one finger and patted
him gently on the back.
"We're so sorry," she
said. "Please don't cry."

The man looked up at their big faces, and smiling sadly through his tears he said,

"I'm sorry if I seem to lay the blame outside your door.
In truth what's happening at home is worrying me more."

"But who are you?" said Vanya, "and where is home?"

"Please forgive my manners, I'm forgetting them, as you see
I'm Theodore, the village bard, my home's beneath this tree."

He pointed to the tree stump he was standing next to, and

*the children saw that there was a tiny wooden door cut into
the side of it.*

"A staircase leads from this tree stump to our hidden village
We Underdwellers live there, safe from predators and pillage."

*"Really?" said Vanya. "Your village is under the ground?"
Theodore nodded.*

"Aye indeed, beneath your feet, great happiness once was found
Our village was a joyous place, where friendship did abound.
Casper and Polonius, twin brothers, ruled us all
And once a month held parties in their great banquet hall.

The whole village was invited, and we danced and sang all night
Till one month fair Alucia came, and oh what a beauteous sight!
Her golden hair fell round her face as she began her singing
And golden notes flew from her throat and filled us all
                                                    with longing.

As Casper watched Alucia, his face with love burned red
But when he told her how he felt, she sadly shook her head.
In the weeks that followed, he tried hard to win her heart
But fair Alucia spurned his love, as she had from the start.

Poor Casper's heart was broke in two, but when a month
                                                    had passed
The time had come for yet another party like the last.
Imagine Casper's horror, when at the party Polonius said
That he and Alucia were in love and soon they would be wed.

Casper cursed his brother, to the wedding he would not go
He waited instead, outside their house, pacing to and fro.
When Polonius and his wife returned, he would not let them in
'You are no longer my brother,' he said, 'from now on I have
                                                        no kin.'

'This house is mine as well as yours,' Polonius was heard
                                                        to shout
There's nowhere else for us to go, you cannot keep us out.'
Casper knew that this was true, he had to let them in
So this he did, and straight away the fighting did begin.

They raged and roared for days and days, brother against brother
And all the villagers took sides, for one or for the other.
Now our village is a place of sadness and of sorrow
And so I weep for good times gone and troubles of tomorrow."

*"But surely if Polonius and his wife moved to a different
house, then the arguments would stop," Maroosia said.
Theodore shook his head as he replied:*

"It takes many years to build a house, with everyone
                                                working together.
So the way things are at the moment, such a task would
                                                go on forever."

*Vanya and Maroosia looked at one another, and their blue
eyes sparkled as they smiled. "We could help," they said, "it
would be easy for us."*
"We could build it under this tree stump," Maroosia said,

97

and she went over to a second broken stump that stood next to the one with the little door in it. "Help me get it loose, Vanya."

Together they worked their fingers into the soil beneath the roots of the stump, and they loosened the earth all around it. Vanya found a thick branch that had fallen from one of the trees, and Maroosia helped him to push one end of it in under the stump. They balanced the middle of the branch on a stone and used it to lever the stump away from the ground. The whole thing rose up then, with a carpet of roots and earth still clinging to it, leaving a circle of bare soil on the forest floor.

Theodore stood up and clapped his hands.

"Now I see your plan," he cried, "a house for one of the brothers. What a wonderful idea, I must go and tell the others."

He disappeared through the little door. Soon Vanya and Maroosia heard the chatter of many excited voices, and a crowd of tiny people made their way out of the tree stump and stood in front of the children. Most of them were dressed in shades of green or brown, like Theodore, but at the head of the crowd stood a couple wearing rich coloured clothes of silk and velvet. Theodore stepped forward.

"May I introduce Polonius, one of our great leaders, Also his wife Alucia, and some villagers willing to help us."

Polonius and Alucia bowed, and all the little villagers bowed too. Vanya and Maroosia explained their idea and everyone set to work straight away. The tiny Underdwellers drew out plans for the new house in the earth with sticks, and the children used sharp flat stones to dig out all the rooms. As the work progressed, more and more of the villagers came out of the door in the tree stump and joined in. They stamped on the floors with their tiny feet to pack the soil, and they wove carpets from long strands of grass. They used their knives to whittle sticks and nut shells into miniature tables and chairs, and they made fireplaces from pebbles that Maroosia collected for them. A tunnel was dug between the new house and the old village. More Underdwellers came through it, to marvel at what had been done in this short time and to help with the work. At last, everyone in the village was working together to finish the house. Only Polonius' brother Casper had not yet appeared.

It was growing dark when the house was finished, and Polonius declared to all the villagers that there was to be a party in the new hall. The Underdwellers went back to their own homes to fetch candle-lit lamps, musical instruments, and plates of delicious food. Vanya and Maroosia sat cross-legged on the ground and watched the musicians playing their harps and flutes and fiddles as the other villagers danced and sang in the light of the tiny lamps. With a sudden bang, the door that joined the new hall to the village opened, and the musicians and villagers stopped what they were doing and fell silent. Standing in the doorway was a little man dressed in clothes of silk and velvet.

"Casper, my brother!" Polonius cried. "You are welcome indeed."

Casper looked slowly round the room at all the faces turned towards him then he went over to Polonius and shook his hand. "Congratulations on your new home," he said gruffly. "I hope you'll both be happy in it."

Theodore climbed up to where Vanya and Maroosia were sitting.

"Did you see that?" *he asked, with a grin.* "Now everything
will be alright
And really it's all thanks to you that they no longer fight.
We're very pleased to have met you, and we hope that when
The time is right you'll both come back and visit us again."

"Oh, we will," said Vanya and Maroosia. "We certainly will, but for now I wonder if you might help us find our way back home. Our grandfather must surely be worried."

Theodore nodded and climbed back down into the new hall to fetch one of the tiny lamps. He hushed the musicians and announced to the Underdwellers that the children were about to go, before climbing back up beside them. All the villagers cheered and shouted their goodbyes as Vanya and Maroosia lowered the tree stump and its carpet of roots back into place over the new house.

"There now," said Maroosia. "You would never know what was hidden away under there."

"Come," said Vanya, "time to go home," and the two children took each other by the hand and followed Theodore's tiny lamp as it bobbed and weaved all the way through the forest, back to their grandfather in the little wooden hut.'

Old Peter gave this big sigh and he laid doon the golden feather. He bent taewards the hearth for his pipe and filled it up wi some baccy fae a leather pouch in his waistcoat pocket. Vanya and Maroosia moved taewards the edge ae the table, and knelt doon tae keek at the totsy green hut and the forest roond it. I went and knelt beside them, and when I bent forward I felt a bit ae a breeze and heard the pine trees shivering in the wind.

Old Peter sat back in his chair and watched us. Then he raised his arms in the air and clapped his hands and the titchy hoose and forest went all shimmery and weird, and then it kind ae sucked itself intae a thin cloud and drifted up intae the air, pirling and spiralling aboot, then whooshing in a stream ae green across the room and intae one ae the green books oan the shelf. 'Grandfather,' went Maroosia as we all gawped at the green light seeping oot fae between the pages ae the book, 'have you told that story before? I feel I know it.'

Her grandfather shook his heid. 'No, little pigeon,' he said, 'it is a new tale. But every story ever told is only the top layer of many older stories. All storytellers learn how to tell tales by having other stories told to them, so there are always echoes of the old stories in the new tales they tell.'

'Wow,' I said. 'I wish I could tell stories like that, stories that made pictures.' Ma voice cracked when the words came oot ma mooth and I realised they were the first I'd spoken in a long while.

The auld man laughed. 'Ah, but you can, little pigeon,' he said. 'You can because you are a storyteller. We all have special things buried inside us, different things that help us make our way in the world, and yours is a gift for telling tales. All you need to do now is to share them. Vanya,' he said, 'some more parchment, please.'

Vanya went back tae the cupboard behind the tapestry and took oot some mair ae the curling yellow paper. He didnae bring it tae his grandfather this time but, he brung it ower tae me. 'Eh . . . thanks,' I went as he pushed the rough crackly paper intae ma hands.

'Write your own story on this paper,' Old Peter said, 'and when it is complete, take it into a bookshop or a library. Choose a book carefully. Find one that is full of other stories, beautiful and exciting and dangerous tales, and hide your story between the pages of this book. You will find that your story will join with the book, become another story for children to read. And the words will be magic, as all words are when they are shared. The children will see them on the page, the words will go in through their eyes, and once they are inside the children, they will turn into pictures and thoughts and feelings. They will act themselves out in the children's heads.' The auld man laid his hand on ma shoulder. 'Goodbye, little pigeon,' he said. 'Good-bye, and remember to share your words.'

'Thanks,' I said. 'Thanks for . . . for everything.'

Vanya and Maroosia walked wi me tae the foot ae the

stairs. Maroosia climbed up in front and pushed open the wooden door. I went past her intae the library.

'Come again,' she said. 'Come back and hear another story.'

'Really?' I went. 'I can come back?'

'Whenever you like,' she says. 'Just knock on the door.'

I waved goodbye and walked oot ae the library, holding the parchment tight in ma hands. I started tae run. The rain had stopped and there wis watery sunlight in the puddles that splintered and sparkled as I stamped through them. Up in the sky above the grey hooses was a bonny big rainbow. I seen ma da and Mary walking in front ae me as I ran along Muirhouse Drive. 'Hi Da,' I shouted oan ma way past them, and ma voice wis stronger this time, my throat no as dry.

'Hello, Jenny love,' he called after me. I ran oan tae oor flat.

I shut the front door wi a bang and walked intae the sitting room just as Jade came oot the kitchenette. 'Where have you been?' she went.

'Tae the library,' I said, and her mooth fell open when she heard me speaking.

I looked at her standing there and then I ran and gave her a big hug.

She laughed and ruffled ma hair. 'Nutter,' she said. She turned her heid and shouted intae the kitchenette, 'Hey Ma, come and listen tae this.'

103

Ma ma appeared, pulling off a pair ae rubber gloves and chucking them ontae the coffee table. The clean and tidy coffee table! 'Hi Ma,' I went. 'Have you been cleaning?'

'Aye,' ma ma said, 'and you're speaking again!' She came rushing over and put her arms roond the baith ae us and kissed the top ae oor heids. She sighed. 'I'm dead lucky, you ken that?' she said.

'How, Ma?' I asked.

'Well, I've got two gorgeous bairns to share ma life wi, haven't I?' she said. She put her hand intae her jeans pocket. 'And by the way, look what I found when I wis cleaning.' She pulled oot the wee-est Russian doll.

I went, 'Brilliant!' and I took it fae her and ran intae the bedroom. I got all the other dolls off ae the windae-sill and I fixed them back thegither roond the totsy one. I gied them a shake and instead ae a hollow rattle there wis a solid thud, like a single heartbeat. I smiled and put them back oan the windae-sill then I sat doon at the desk wi ma parchment. I thought aboot what Old Peter had telt me and I got dead excited, imagining the sort ae bairns that might read ma story, bairns like me. I wondered what I could make up for them, what I could possibly tell them that would be interesting tae hear. Then it came tae me. 'Hey!' I wrote. 'Listen tae this. I'm gonnae tell you a secret . . .'

THE SMILE

ALISON PRINCE

I'm getting on the bus with the others. We're going to spend a day at the new High School, to see what's it's like before we start there next term.

SIT THERE, BY THE WINDOW.

I sit where Buddy tells me. I expect he has chosen the best place. He is always right.

CORRECT. YOU ARE LUCKY. REMEMBER, YOU ARE LUCKY.

I know. You keep telling me.

GOOD.

I'm looking out of the window, watching the other kids get on the bus. A girl looks up and waves at me.

DO NOT WAVE BACK.

I'd put my hand up to wave, but I put it down again.

The school we're going to is only just finished. They've

been building it for nearly two years, on the grassy bit just past the Scottish Parliament. I can see the Scottish Parliament—

NOT POSSIBLE. THE SCOTTISH PARLIAMENT IS 3.87 MILES FROM HERE.

I can see it if I shut my eyes, because I've seen it before. It has all those curvy bits of pale wood across the front, like the designer was thinking of a forest.

CONTROL YOUR MIND. UNREAL OBSERVATIONS ARE NOT USEFUL.

Sorry.

APOLOGY ACCEPTED. REMEMBER, YOU ARE LUCKY.

The girl who waved has come to sit on the empty seat beside me. The bus is full, so someone had to. The girl's name is Margaret, but the other kids call her Midge. I would call her Midge, too, if I spoke to her, but I don't speak to the Ordinaries much. She kneels on the seat the wrong way round so as to talk to the girl behind her.

Mrs Armit says, 'Margaret, sit down, the bus is starting.'

Midge flops down and sighs. She puts one foot on top of the seat in front, but takes it down again when the teacher looks at her. The bus engine makes a shaking noise. Now it's settled into a roar. We're moving off.

FASTEN YOUR SEATBELT.

I fasten my seatbelt.

Mrs Armit says, 'Good boy, Meko. Everybody, put your seat belts on.'

Midge looks at me. She says, 'How come you always get things right?'

Nobody has ever asked me that. I don't know what to say.

I'M JUST LUCKY, Buddy tells me.

'I'm just lucky.'

'You're not lucky, you're weird,' Midge says. 'Don't you know that?'

DO NOT ANSWER.

She's rushing on, so I don't have to answer.

'I mean, you're so kind of perfect,' she says. 'I'm not getting at you or anything, but you seem like – I don't know – like you think we're all idiots.'

SMILE. SAY, 'I DON'T THINK THAT AT ALL'.

I haven't practised smiling lately.

CORNERS OF THE MOUTH UP. YOU KNOW HOW.

Corners of the mouth up, OK. I start to say, 'I don't think that at—' but she interrupts.

'Why can't you smile as if you mean it?' she says.

This puzzles me. I ask, 'What is a smile supposed to mean?'

UNSANCTIONED QUESTION. BE CAREFUL.

Sometimes I wish Buddy would shut up.

UNSANCTIONED THOUGHT, he says more loudly. **BE CAREFUL.**

'It means you think something is funny,' Midge is saying. 'Or it could mean you like someone.'

I can't see how turning the corners of your mouth up can mean two different things. Maybe they are not different. I ask, 'Is funny the same as liking someone?'

UNSANCTIONED! Buddy is getting really cross now. He'll punish me in a minute, but I don't care.

YOU MUST CARE. BE CAREFUL.

Midge is laughing. 'That's sweet,' she says.

'How is it sweet?'

STOP!

I can't stop. Sweets come in wrappers, or in bright packets, so what does she mean? This is so interesting.

'Sweet is like, nice.' She shifts to look at me better, and folds her arms. 'You're not quite *right*, are you. Do you have an illness or something?'

STOP THIS CONVERSATION!

Midge has asked a question, so I need to answer it.

Buddy quietens down. TELL HER, 'I HAD A BRAIN INJURY WHEN I WAS YOUNG'.

'I had a brain injury when I was young.'

'You poor thing,' says Midge. 'That's what happened to Martin, when he was born. That's why he's got cerebral palsy.'

Martin can't manage his arms and legs, and talking is difficult for him.

'I'm not like that,' I say. 'I'm perfectly well.'

'Then what is it?' asks Midge.

STOP.

I don't know how to stop.

SAY, 'IT'S NOTHING'.

'It's nothing.'

But it is something, of course. It's Buddy. I used to think everyone had a Buddy, but when I started school Uncle Oliver told me they don't. He said I had to mix with the Ordinaries, so as to learn how to handle them. I don't think I can handle them yet. They get things wrong a lot because they don't have a Buddy to tell them what to do. They use mobile phones and music and noise to fill the emptiness in their heads. Most of them muck about a lot, because they are not special. Just Ordinaries.

'You can't say it's nothing,' Midge is going on. 'You're not like – well – normal, are you.' She puts her hand on my sleeve and gazes at me seriously. 'What is it? You must know.'

LOOK OUT OF THE WINDOW, THEN SHE WILL BE QUIET. Buddy sounds calmer now. I think he knows it's not my fault she started talking to me.

CORRECT. BUT DO AS I SAY. LOOK OUT OF THE WINDOW.

I look out of the window. He is right, Midge has shut up, but she is still looking at me. I can see her face in the glass, behind mine. She has long dark hair, very curly and untidy. Mine is even darker than hers, silky black, but it is cut short. My eyes are black, too. The Ordinaries are very rude if they catch me in the playground when

109

the teacher is not looking. They push the corners of their eyes up and stick their tongues out, and shout, 'Jappy, Jappy, dirty nappy'. I asked the teacher to tell them it is rude, but it made them worse. They shove me about and trip me up, and one of them broke my ruler.

DO NOT THINK ABOUT THOSE THINGS.

No. I will concentrate on what is outside. There are buildings going past. Now there's a tree, very tall, a deep green colour, with feathery leaves. I like trees, they don't talk. They are just themselves.

THAT IS NOT A REASON FOR LIKING THEM.

I shut my eyes and lean my forehead on the glass, but the jiggling of the bus makes it uncomfortable. I turn away from the window.

'Did you have an accident?' Midge asks. 'Or was it one of those birth things like with Martin – you know, when the baby can't get out properly?'

SAY IT WAS AN ACCIDENT.

'It was an accident.'

'So what happened?'

YOU DON'T KNOW.

'I don't know.' I'm going on without waiting for Buddy. 'I don't remember. I must have been quite small.'

UNNECESSARY. SAY, 'I DON'T WANT TO TALK ABOUT IT'.

But I do want to talk about it.

DO **NOT** TALK ABOUT IT. **THIS IS AN ORDER.**

'Do you have brothers and sisters?' Midge asks.

110

'No.' I'm not sure if this is right. Uncle Oliver says there are other Specials like me, but I don't know them.

DO NOT TALK.

'Where do you live, anyway?' Midge asks. 'I know you come in that big car every morning, and it takes you home, but where's your house?'

DO NOT ANSWER.

'Near the University.'

UNAUTHORISED ANSWER. BE CAREFUL – YOU WILL BE PUNISHED.

The House looks like the others in the old terrace. Black railings, wide stone steps up to a front door painted dark blue. But inside, it's very light and modern.

'Dead posh area,' says Midge.

'Posh?'

UNAUTHORISED.

'You know – classy,' says Midge. 'No barbed wire or boarded-up windows and stuff.'

'The House has tall windows, with shutters inside,' I tell her. 'There's a half-circle window above the front door, with coloured glass in a pattern.'

STOP THIS AT ONCE!

Buddy will give me a punishment in a minute. It's going to hurt, but I'm too interested to stop. Am I posh? The Ordinaries are not posh. Sometimes they fight in the playground and hurt each other. One of them got so hurt last week that he covered his face with his hands and made a noise, and water came out of his eyes. They call it crying. I would like to know what crying is.

PUNISHMENT! PUNISHMENT!

Alarm bells shriek in my mind, and the pain starts, a burning stab. I've made a noise, too, because it's worse than I expected. My hands have clutched at the top of my head.

Midge grabs at my sleeve. 'Meko, what is it?' But the pain has stopped.

SAY, 'IT WAS NOTHING. I'M ALL RIGHT'.

'It was nothing. I'm all right.'

Her eyes are staring into mine. I think she is trying to understand. I wish I could explain.

BE CAREFUL, Buddy warns. **LOOK AWAY, OUT OF THE WINDOW.**

I look away, out of the window.

Trees go by. I am seeing them without words.

Just seeing them.

Just seeing them.

*

The bus is stopping. We are outside a big school that doesn't look quite finished. It's very white, and it's made of peculiar shapes, a bit like the Scottish Parliament. Inside the tall windows, I can see big grey machines. I don't know what they are.

THAT IS A FITNESS SUITE, Buddy tells me. THE MACHINES ARE FOR ORDINARIES TO EXERCISE ON, BECAUSE MANY OF THEM ARE FAT AND UNHEALTHY. THE MACHINES WITH SEATS ARE LIKE BOATS, FOR ROWING. THE ONES WITH BELTS TO PUT YOUR FEET ON ARE TREADMILLS.

Midge says, 'It looks like a torture chamber!'

'It's a fitness suite,' I tell her. 'Those are treadmills and rowing machines.'

'That's what I mean about you,' she says. 'You know everything. It's creepy.'

TELL HER YOU SAW IT ON TV.

'I saw it on TV.'

'Oh, right. Do you have a TV in your room?'

SAY YES.

'Yes.'

'My mum won't let me. She says it stops you from using your imagination.'

DO NOT ANSWER.

The teacher is calling everyone together, so I don't have to answer.

The TV in my room is not the kind that Midge sees. My TV brings me Uncle Oliver. I can never see Buddy, so it's nice to have someone real in my room. The school has Ordinary TV, but it is stupid.

*

We are walking down a long corridor. The doors are a dark red colour, with grey bands round them, but the

113

walls and ceiling are pure white. There are diggers and fork-lift trucks outside, and it's all muddy, but in here, the floors are made of pale wood and everything is very clean. Jimmy Mack nudges his friend and makes a hissing noise, pointing his hand at the wall as if he is holding something with his finger pressing the top of it.

'He would, wouldn't he,' says Midge.

I don't know what she means.

She moves her own hand like the boy did, then says, 'Spray can. Graffiti.'

DO NOT ASK ANY MORE.

Midge has gone to talk to some other girls. I am alone again.

GOOD.

*

We have been shown the labs for chemistry, physics and biology. They are very much like the lab in The House, only bigger. Now we are in a computer suite. None of this is new to me. Really, it's quite boring.

I was born in The House. Uncle Oliver says I was created in perfect conditions. That is why I don't have what the Ordinaries call a belly-button. Ordinaries come out of Ordinary mothers, and the button is where the cord that joined them came off. And nobody equips them with a Buddy in the brain as they did for me.

YOU ARE LUCKY, Buddy reminds me.

I once heard someone in The House refer to Buddy as

'the chip'. The Ordinaries think a chip is a piece of fried potato, but that may be what they call a joke.

CORRECT. THAT IS WHAT THEY CALL IT.

We are in the Home Economics suite. There are a lot of cookers, both gas and electric, and microwaves and washing machines. Midge is beside me again. She asks, 'Do you like it here?'

SAY YES.

'Yes.'

She seems not to be satisfied.

'Meko, I want to know what you *really* think!'

She is staring at me hard. Her eyes are grey, with dark eyelashes, and she is not smiling. This is interesting. If a smile means something is funny, like she said, then not smiling means something is not funny.

WALK AWAY. TELL HER YOU NEED TO GO TO THE TOILET.

I don't need to go to the toilet. I want to stay here.

DO AS YOU ARE TOLD.

If her question is not funny, then it must be serious. Does this mean a smile shows you are not serious? She said it could show that you like someone, too. So not being serious is something to like. That seems odd, but it's quite nice.

There's a buzzing sound in my head. **WARNING – IRRATIONAL INPUT MAY ENDANGER THE SYSTEM.** Buddy's voice is very loud. **WALK AWAY. WALK AWAY NOW.**

But I'm busy. 'Please,' I say to Midge, 'show me how to smile.'

She stares at me and says, 'You're kidding. Everyone knows how to smile.'

'I don't.'

'You poor thing. How can I tell you . . . ' I can see she is thinking hard.

Buddy is still shouting **WALK AWAY, WALK AWAY!**

I'm scared about what he's going to do to me in a minute, and it's hard to hear Midge for all the noise he's making, but I can if I concentrate.

'It's a kind of warm feeling,' she's saying. 'It comes up from somewhere near your tummy. You get it in your throat and behind your eyes, and it makes your mouth feel sort of bigger. Your lips curve up because they just have to. Because you're happy.'

WALK AWAY NOW, OR YOU WILL BE PUNISHED.

'Try it, Meko.' Midge has put her fingers to the side of my face, quite lightly. It is the first time an Ordinary has touched me in that sort of way. They usually poke or shove. She is smiling. 'Go on. Just be happy.'

NO! NO!

But a smile has grown without me telling it to, and it is so funny that I don't know what to do with it. I want to hide it with my hands, but I can't. I'm smiling, and I feel wonderful.

PUNISHMENT! PUNISHMENT!

The alarm screams in my ears. The pain is more than I have ever known. I am doubled over, holding my head. I can't breathe.

Midge is shouting for the teacher.

'Mrs Armit, quick, there's something the matter with Meko!'

It's stopped. **STAND UP**, says Buddy. **QUICKLY**.

Mrs Armit comes hurrying over. 'Meko, what is it?' she asks.

IT'S NOTHING.

'It's nothing.'

'If you are not well, I'll phone your uncle.'

SAY, 'IT'S ALL RIGHT'. Buddy's voice has quietened, but it sounds scratchy and hoarse.

'It's all right.'

IT WAS A JOKE.

'It was a joke.'

Mrs Armit's mouth has gone kind of tight. 'I am surprised at you,' she says. 'You, of all people, Meko. We are in a special place, on our best behaviour. You are letting all of us down.'

Midge says, 'It's my fault. I thought he had a pain.' She looks at me out of her grey eyes, and she is not smiling.

Mrs Armit turns away. She is not smiling, either. She glances at her watch, then calls out, 'Listen, everyone, it's time for lunch. We are going into the Junior Recreation Area. Your lunch boxes will be waiting for you there.'

*

117

The Junior Recreation Area is meant for smaller children, because there is going to be a nursery school here as well. It has bouncy things that look like horses, and there are square patterns marked in coloured paint for the game they call Peevers. There is a small house, too, not much taller than I am. Most of the girls have crowded into it. Midge said it's a Wendy House. I don't know what that means.

IT HAS NO MEANING. Buddy's voice still sounds cracked and scratchy.

Anyway, Midge is in the Wendy House, too. I have found a sand-pit. I am drawing in the sand with my finger. Drawing is good, it has no words.

DRAWING IS NOT NECESSARY.

I know.

YOU MAY DO IT FOR A WHILE.

Thank you.

Midge has come out of the Wendy House. She looks across and sees me. I go on drawing.

She has come to stand beside me. She looks at my drawing and says, 'Trees.'

I look at her, but I don't say anything.

'There's something weird, isn't there,' she says.

I can't tell her, but I give a very small nod, like the Ordinaries do when they mean Yes.

Now Midge is drawing, too.

She's drawn a stick-man. She's

118

written 'Meko' beside it. She's drawing a big dot inside his head. She is looking at me. I know what she is asking.

'Yes,' I say, stupidly.

ILLOGICAL. NO QUESTION WAS ASKED.

Midge is not smiling. She touches my forehead with her finger, and waits for an answer.

I nod.

YOU MUST USE WORDS.

Midge puts her finger and thumb together beside my head as if picking something out and flicks it away, then holds her hands palms up. Can you get rid of it? Her eyes and mine seem joined, we are looking at each other so hard. She is waiting for an answer.

I shake my head as the Ordinaries do when they mean No.

She covers her face with her hands.

*

Uncle Oliver is on my TV screen. He always comes when Buddy has helped me with my homework and logged off for recharge.

'I see from Buddy's log that you had two punishments this afternoon,' he says. He always knows.

'Yes. I'm sorry.'

His hair is short and black, like mine. He wears thick glasses that make his eyes look as big as pools of water. They are very pale, bright blue.

'You know how special you are,' he says. 'Don't you.'

119

'Yes. I am lucky.'

'There are very few of you Special children,' he goes on. 'Only seventeen in the whole world. I hope you will not let us down.'

I shake my head.

'Don't do that,' he says sharply. 'It's a sloppy habit that you've picked up from the Ordinaries. Use proper words.'

'Sorry. No, I will not let you down.'

'Buddy is your friend. He helps you to think clearly and logically.'

'Yes.'

'But he cannot work with things that are not expressed in words. Your disobedience today has done him quite a lot of damage.'

'I'm sorry.' But I am seeing Midge's smile.

Uncle takes his glasses off. His pale eyes look quite small without them. He wipes the lenses carefully on a small yellow cloth, then puts his glasses back on, and his eyes look large again.

'Do you know why the Ordinaries have become so stupid?' he asks.

I almost shake my head, but remember that I mustn't. 'No,' I say, 'not really.'

'They think their feelings matter. They want to feel good and nice all the time, although they almost never do. They are sentimental, so they never think logically. They cannot face the fact that they sometimes have to do hard or difficult things. They are afraid of ever being uncomfortable.'

I think of Jimmy Mack. 'Some of them like being stupid,' I say. But Midge is not like that.

'Exactly,' Uncle is saying. 'You, Meko, are lucky to be punished when you make a mistake, because it helps you to learn. The Ordinaries want everything to be easy, so they say their children are all right, even when they are all wrong.'

I say, 'Yes, I see.'

'And of course, Ordinary children have no Buddy to tell them what they should do,' Uncle goes on. 'And neither do their parents. A few of them are quite intelligent, despite that, and they can be dangerous, because they do not bow to superior logic.'

'Right.' I don't quite know what he means. I keep seeing Midge looking at me and not smiling.

Uncle Oliver is not smiling either, but then he never does.

'We will have to work all night on Buddy,' he says, 'because you damaged him.'

'I'm sorry.'

'I should hope so. Any more disobedience may cause a fatal overload. Do you know what that means?'

'Not really.'

'It means Buddy may not work any more. And if that happens, you will be of no further use to us. You will have failed your system test. And worse, you will have destroyed all that we are trying to do.'

My mouth feels dry. I think I'm what they call scared.

'Why do you think we sent you to the school?' Uncle goes on.

'You said it was to learn how to handle the Ordinaries.'

His pale blue eyes are staring at me very hard.

'That is correct. But there is something you have to understand, Meko. When you were created, we had to use an Ordinary human ovum – that means egg – so as to provide you with a body that can do all the Ordinary things. But there is a danger. It may turn out that you are not the right carrier for Buddy. That is why we have to run this series of tests, to make sure your superior logic is proof against any Ordinary instincts. I am telling you this so that you can guard against non-logical behaviour. Do you understand?'

I've always tried to get things right, I want to please him. I say, 'You mean I must try harder.'

'You must indeed,' he agrees. 'All emotion is dangerous, because it is non-logical. Today, you have seen the damage an uncontrolled smile can cause. Laughter is capable of blowing circuits. And above all, beware of tears.'

There is something I have to ask, though I don't want to.

'Must I keep away from Midge?'

'Yes,' says Uncle Oliver. 'That above all. Keep well away. She is very dangerous.'

*

122

I have kept away from Midge all morning. At playtime, I ran about near the other boys and pretended I was in their game. I saw her watching, but I did not look at her. Now it is afternoon break. I am near the boys again, but they do not want me.

Jimmy Mack says, 'Shove off, slitty-eyed twit.'

'Stinky Chink,' says another.

They hold their noses and make 'Ying-tong, ying-tong' noises, and poke me with their fingers.

Mrs Armit has gone inside with a girl who had grazed her knee. The boys are close round me now. They are pushing me hard, shoving me about. I try to stand firm, but a thump in my back sends me pitching forward. I don't know what to do.

WALK AWAY, says Buddy.

But there's no way out. One of the boys smacks me in the head. Another boots me behind the knees. I'm on the ground. They are kicking me.

'Leave him alone!' someone yells. It's Midge. She is battering at the boys, screaming at them. They turn on her, and I get to my feet.

WALK AWAY, WALK AWAY—

They are pulling her hair, saying she's my girlfriend, calling her a rotten slag. Some of the other girls have come over, but they just shout at the boys and don't do anything. I'm trying to haul one of the boys away, because I'm scared they might hurt Midge. He elbows me in the stomach, and I double up.

123

WA—AWAY! WA—WAY!

Buddy's voice is breaking up, but I can't listen. The boys are very strong. Two of them have grabbed me, they are forcing my arms up behind my back. The girls have gone running in, screaming for Mrs Armit.

YOU – BE – PUN – SH –

Midge turns to run, but Jimmy Mack trips her and she falls. Her head hits the tarmac very hard. She's lying still, with her arms sprawled out.

Jimmy pokes her with his foot and says, 'Don't arse about – get up.' But she doesn't move.

The boys all run away and start a game near the climbing frame.

I kneel beside Midge. There is blood coming out of her nose. It is dribbling down into her dark hair.

Mrs Armit is behind me. 'Oh, my goodness,' she says. 'Kelly, go and get Mr McIver, quickly.'

I put my hand to Midge's face, but her eyes do not open. I think she is dead.

PUN — SH — ME — T!

The alarm screams. Pain is blasting my head, but there's another pain gathering in my chest. It rises to my throat in a huge ache, and my eyes sting with a hot wetness that mixes with the howling noise I am making and overflows down my face.

'Oh, Meko,' says Mrs Armit, 'it's all right, we'll take care of her. Don't cry.'

*

The light outside the window is pale green. Everything is blurred. I shut my eyes.

I've opened them again. Better.

There is this pattern of green things, with thin lines between them. They sparkle in the brightness. I like them.

Tree.

Yes, it is called Tree. I'm almost sure that's right.

Somehow, I can't stay awake.

*

Someone has picked up my wrist. Fingers hold it for a few moments, pressing gently, then tuck my hand back under the covers.

Whoever it is says, 'Hi – talk to me a minute?'

I open my eyes. There's whiteness, close to me. It's a white coat. The man wearing it is sitting beside my bed. He has red hair, quite curly.

'How's the head?' he asks.

I'm not sure. It aches a bit, but it feels very quiet and peaceful. I put my hand up to touch it. Why is my head all wrapped up?

'Good,' says the man, 'you're hearing me. You've had an operation, but I don't think you know about that. You were in quite a bad way.'

I look across at the window. Outside, it is still green and sparkly. I want to tell the man about the tree, because he seems nice. I'm trying to make my tongue move.

'T—' it says. 'T—'

I take another breath and try again.

'Tree.'

'Hey, that's brilliant!' he says. 'Tree, yes, just outside the window. Well done! You go back to sleep now. I'll see you tomorrow.'

*

This must be tomorrow.

'I'm called Tom,' the man with curly hair says. 'Doctor Tom, but Tom will do. Can you say "Tom"?'

'T— Tom.'

'Great. And you are Meko, right?'

Meko-rite? It sounds funny. There are other words like that. Meteorite. Meteorbike. It's fast and shiny, very loud, and the rider is leaning forward. His hands are in big, black gloves, and he wears a red helmet. Not meteorbike. Motorbike. Yes, that's it. I'll tell Tom.

'Mo—' The sounds won't come, but I'm trying hard. 'Mo— ike.'

'Mike?' Tom asks. 'Is that what your friends call you? OK, that's fine. Listen, Mike, you're a bit of a mystery. You have an address on the school register, but the house is empty. Nobody answers the phone. E-mails bounce. Can you tell me where you live?'

I am new. I can't answer. I live here.

*

It's another tomorrow.

'Hi, Mike,' says Tom. 'This came in the post. Looks like someone's sent you a present.'

He puts a flat package on my bed. I'm trying to open it, but my fingers don't work very well.

'Want a hand?' asks Tom.

'Yes. Please.' I'm getting better at talking.

He opens the brown envelope. A thin drawing book slides out. There's a piece of paper clipped to the front, with lines of pencil writing on it. I don't know how to understand them, but I think they mean something.

Tom asks, 'Shall I read you what it says?'

'Yes.'

He picks up the piece of paper. 'It's from someone called Midge. She says, "Hi, Meko. I did these drawings for you. They are about you. I don't know if I got it right about the way things are, but I hope you are OK. I'm fine now, but I had to stay in bed for three days. The boys got told off. Jimmy Mack got suspended but he said it was great not being at school. I hope you come back to school soon. Love, Midge".'

Midge. I know that word. How do I know it? I can't think of a way to find out.

Tom starts turning the pages, one at a time.

The book has coloured pictures in it, very carefully

drawn. The first one is a boy. Now there's a big hand coming from the top of the page, with a black dot held in its fingers.

Next page. The dot is in the boy's head. The hand is still above him.

The page turns again. The boy has fallen down. Zigzags are coming out of his head. Now the boy is with a lot of other boys, all round him. There is fighting. Now a drawing of a white van with a yellow stripe along the side.

The boy is lying on a table. There are big lights above the table, and people are standing round it. One of them has a knife.

Now the boy is in bed.

Tom whistles quietly. 'This is amazing,' he says. 'Midge, whoever she is, knows something we don't, I think. We'll have to talk to her. Can you remember her, Mike?'

Midge. Midge. I'm trying so hard, but I can't—

'Never mind,' says Tom. 'She gives her address, we'll get in touch with her. The thing is, Mike, she may be right. We operated on you because the scan showed a blood clot in your brain, but you'll never guess what was in the middle of the clot. An electronic chip.'

*

A girl has come, with her mother. They are talking to Doctor Tom, but the girl keeps looking across at me. She comes over and sits beside me. Her hair is curly like

128

Tom's, but long and dark. She is looking at me very carefully.

'It's gone, hasn't it,' she says.

I feel as if there are things I must tell her, but I don't know what they are.

'I'm . . . new,' I say.

She nods slowly. 'Yes. I can see. Are you all right?'

I look out of the window. The tree is holding up its leaves in the sun, and they are sparkling. I like them a lot. I'm looking back at the girl.

'Happy,' I tell her. 'I am happy.'

She smiles.

I know this smile. I know it, I know it—

Yes. She is my friend. She is called Midge. I feel warm all over, from my toes right up to my quiet, peaceful head, and Midge's smile is my smile, too. It is spreading all over my face.

'That's OK, then,' says Midge.

Somehow, this is funny.

The smile we are sharing grows into laughter.

Doctor Tom and the woman turn their heads to look at us. They both seem astonished.

Outside, the leaves are sparkling
in the sun.

It is all so lovely that I laugh
and laugh.

Friends Forever

CATHY CASSIDY

It's one of those hot, sunny days you sometimes get in May, the kind of day when school drags on forever and all you really want to do is be outside. You want the feel of grass under your bare feet, the cool slide of sun cream on hot shoulders, the warmth and the laughter and the drifts of soft, pink cherry blossom on every pavement.

It is a perfect day to turn eleven.

I've brought in punnets of strawberries to share with my classmates, and Miss McCall lets us eat them at our desks, so our lips are stained scarlet and the sweet juice drips down on to our spelling test papers.

'I can't wait,' Mina Khalid whispers. 'I just cannot *wait* until the picnic!'

'How can we concentrate on spellings and fractions and guitar lessons when the sun is beating down out there?' Joe Tyler says. 'It's cruel!'

'At least your guitar lesson got you out of science,' I point out.

'But he's right, Lexi, it's too hot to work,' Lia Castelli protests. 'School is pure torture on a day like this!'

The sun is slanting down outside, turning our world rainbow-bright after a long, long winter of grey. We've had months of icy winds and slippery pavements and endless drizzle, and now, almost overnight, it's practically tropical. We can't quite believe it.

Weegie Robson, the naughtiest boy in the class, is claiming he got sunstroke at lunchtime, playing footy with his shirt off. Miss McCall tells him to keep his shirt on in future, and gives him a scoosh of her sun cream and a drink of water from the cooler.

'A birthday picnic,' Mina sighs. 'How cool is that?'

'Cool,' Joe nods.

'Super-cool,' Lia says.

'Mum was up till late last night, baking,' I tell them. 'And there'll be salads and pizza and lemonade . . .'

It was a last-minute plan, really. I'd asked Mina, Lia and Joe round to my house for a birthday tea, but when the weather started to sizzle it seemed crazy to be stuck indoors. Mum said we could have a picnic instead, in Princes Street Gardens, looking up at the castle, and everyone said that sounded just perfect.

When the bell rings at half three, our mums are waiting at the door, laden down with picnic baskets and cool boxes and rolled up rugs. Mina's little brother Kawa is there too, and Lia's sisters, Gina and Mimi. We hurtle out to join them, Joe with his guitar slung over his back in its squishy red case.

We take a bus into town and get off right in the middle

of Princes Street, and Mum buys everyone an ice-cream from the kiosk by the station. A piper is playing opposite Jenners, sweltering in his kilt and jacket as he entertains the tourists. Kawa runs up and asks him to play 'Happy Birthday' for me, and amazingly, he does. Mina, Lia and the little ones start singing along with him, and Joe gets his guitar out and strums along. A little crowd gathers on the pavement, and the piper laughs and tells us to clear off before we swipe all his business.

We leg it out across the grass, weaving in and out of little groups of people soaking up the sun. There are pink-faced teenage girls, giggling and rolling up their shirtsleeves to get a tan, and mothers with pushchairs and grizzling toddlers in sunhats. There are workmen with their T-shirts off, and knots of tourists fanning themselves with guidebooks, and a couple of scruffy blokes drinking whisky, even though it's still the middle of the afternoon.

We choose the space with the best view of the castle, spread our rugs and blankets, and flop down. The mums unpack the picnic feast, cold pizza and potato salad and crisps and fairy cakes and fresh cherries and something called baklava that Mina's mum has made, all filo pastry and nuts and syrup. It's a delicacy in Kurdish Iraq, apparently, where Mina is from originally.

There's cool lemonade, just like I'd predicted, and cola and smoothies, and, of course, my birthday cake, which is iced with chocolate buttercream, and topped with eleven candles.

When we've eaten all we can, Mum lights the candles and everyone sings 'Happy Birthday' again, and I blow the candles out and make a wish.

'What d'you wish for?' Joe wants to know, lying back in the grass. He has peeled off his socks and rolled up his trousers to get a better tan, revealing milk-white legs and freckly feet.

Joe got teased a bit when he first came to our school last year, because he was pale and blond and had one of those English accents that sounds kind of posh if you're not used to it. Miss McCall has a radar for that kind of thing, though. She told us that Edinburgh was like a great big bag of pick 'n' mix, filled with all kinds of people from all over the world. There was room for everyone, here, she said.

'He's not Scottish, though,' Weegie had grumbled. 'Not like us.'

My family were Scottish, right enough. We'd lived in Edinburgh for years and years. I knew that, because Mum was tracing our family tree and she'd got back as far as Victorian times.

'Well, I'm not Scottish, am I?' Mina said, tossing her long, glossy plaits back and flashing her dark eyes at Weegie. 'I lived in Iraq until I was seven!'

'Yeah, but you *talk* like us,' he argued. 'You've got the accent and everything.'

'Well, this is my home now,' Mina said. 'Iraq was not a good place for us Kurds, so we came here. Edinburgh has made us welcome.'

'Like my family,' Lia chipped in. 'They came over from Italy in the 50s, started up a chip shop business. I guess I'm sort of Scottish and Italian!'

'You two are OK,' Weegie admitted. 'I'm not saying you actually have to be born here to belong . . .'

'Were you born here, Weegie?' Mina asked, sweetly.

Weegie's cheeks flushed pink. 'You know I wasn't,' he scowled. 'I came here from Glasgow back in P3, same as you.'

'Exactly,' Mina said, laughing.

'See what I mean?' Miss McCall had said. 'This city is a

134

great big mix-up, and that's what makes it so lively, so special. You're very welcome, Joe . . . seriously.'

'Sure,' Mina said. 'Sit with us, Joe.'

Joe did.

He settled in pretty well after that, but although he liked playing footy and hanging out with the boys, his best friends were Mina and Lia and me. He's OK, for a pale, blond boy with a funny southern accent. More than OK.

'So, what d'you wish for?' he repeats, now, squinting at me from beneath his blond fringe.

When I blew out my birthday candles I wished for this day to go on forever, here in the sunshine in Princes Street Gardens with my three best friends, and our families close by and chocolate cake and the scent of cut grass and happiness.

I don't say that, of course.

'I was wishing you hadn't taken your socks off,' I laugh. 'Pheeew . . . cheesy or what?'

Joe pelts me with the scrunched-up socks, and Mina and Lia jump to my rescue, and the three of us chase Joe round and round the park until he falls to his knees and begs for mercy.

'Lexi, you didn't really make a wish about my socks, did you?' Joe asks.

'Nah. I was wishing the three of you would hurry up and cough up with my pressies!' I tell them.

'You're not supposed to nag us!' Lia says.

'You're supposed to be patient, and mature, and sensible,' Mina agrees. 'After all, you are eleven now!'

I pull a face. 'I don't want to be patient and mature and sensible,' I say.

Joe rolls his eyes. 'Not much chance of that anyway,' he says. 'Still, I suppose we've made you wait long enough. Present time! Here's mine . . .'

Joe chucks me a soft, squashy package wrapped in silvery tissue paper, and I open it up to reveal one of those big chequered scarves with the fringy edging, in black and bright pink. 'Aw, Joe . . . it's brilliant!' I tell him, honestly. 'I love it!'

Lia gives me a tiny parcel with a ring inside. It's small and silver, with a cloudy grey stone.

'It's great!' I say, slipping it on. 'Thanks, Lia!'

'It's a mood ring,' Lia tells me, shaking a tiny folded leaflet out of the wrapping paper. 'See? The stone changes colour to reflect your mood. Blue means sad, pink means happy, red means angry, green means jealous . . .'

As she speaks, the stone dims and glows pink. 'See?' Lia laughs. 'You're happy!'

Mina's present is last. I open it carefully, so as not to spoil the patterned paper, to find a little book about making friendship bracelets and some skeins of coloured thread, pre-cut to length.

'Friendship bracelet threads!' I say. 'Perfect, Mina! Wow!'

My friends fall on Mina's gift, scanning through the booklet, choosing threads. 'Some of the weaves are difficult,' Mina tells us. 'They take a while to master. But we could plait bracelets for each other until we learn the tricky weaves . . .'

She shows us how to select three colours and knot them together at the top. 'I'll hold yours, Lexi,' she tells me. 'You plait. Then tie it onto my wrist . . . that's a friendship bracelet. You are weaving your  friendship into the plait, like a magic charm.'

'You must never cut through a friendship bracelet,' Lia adds, picking out some threads of her own. 'If you do, it cuts through the friendship. It's bad luck!'

'We won't,' I promise her. 'Friends forever, right?'

'Forever,' Mina agrees.

'Definitely,' Lia says.

Joe laughs and rolls his eyes. 'I guess,' he says. 'Forever.'

We sit for an hour, plaiting bracelets and tying them onto each others' wrists until each of us has three bracelets apiece.

The sun is not so warm now. The piper opposite Jenners has packed up for the evening and the crowds are starting to thin. Mum is tidying away the picnic stuff, and the little kids are getting tired and restless.

'Ten minutes,' Mum says. 'And then we'll have to make a move, OK, kids?'

I nod, wishing I could make those ten minutes last forever. Joe is strumming his guitar and singing a Mika song under his breath. Lia is combing through my hair with her fingers, making tiny plaits, and Mina just snaffles the last baklava and lies back on the grass, sighing, with her head in my lap.

As birthdays go, it is pretty much perfect.

The next day, Mina isn't in school.

'Too much baklava,' Joe says, and we just laugh. Later on, I call their flat to talk to Mina, but there's no reply, and Mum says they're probably out or busy, and not to worry. I'm not worrying, exactly. I just want to know if everything's OK.

'She'll be in school tomorrow,' Mum says.

But she isn't, and Joe doesn't make jokes about baklava today. Lia says that Mina's little brother Kawa isn't in school either, and that makes us faintly uneasy. 'It'll be a bug,' I say. 'One of those summer things that wipes you out for a day or two.'

But it turns out that I'm wrong.

After Miss McCall reads through the register, she

138

turns towards us, her face grave. She doesn't mention spelling tests or the nine times table, or whether we have our topic work finished. She just looks at us, her eyes extra bright, as if they might well up with tears at any moment.

'I have bad news,' she tells us. 'Some very bad news, about Mina.'

Joe's smile slips for the first time in the history of the universe, and Lia covers my hand with hers. My mind races, sifting through the list of possible disasters. What could make Miss McCall look so serious, so sad?

'You all know that Mina and her family came to Edinburgh from Iraq,' Miss McCall tells us. 'They were Kurdish refugees – asylum seekers, if you like. They came here because it wasn't safe for them to stay in Iraq. The Kurds were treated very badly by Iraq's old leader, and so our country decided that Mina and her family could stay here, for a while at least.'

There is silence in the classroom, even from Weegie Robson.

'Unfortunately, the authorities have decided that it is now best for some asylum seekers to return to Iraq,' Miss McCall continues. 'The old leader has been removed, and Iraq should now be safer, but . . . '

'Where is Mina?' I ask, my voice shaking. 'What's happened to her?'

Miss McCall bites her lip. 'Lexi, I don't know that for sure,' she replies. 'The school has been told that Mina and her family have been refused long-term asylum status. They were taken to a detention centre down south, early yesterday morning. Unless they can over-turn the decision, they will be deported to Iraq.'

My stomach turns to water. Beside me, Lia is crying quietly, fat salty tears sliding down her cheeks, while Joe is just shaking his head and staring blankly, as if he can't make sense of this. I know how he feels.

Iraq . . . it's a country you see on the news, hot and dusty and hostile, in reports about Allied soldiers being killed by snipers or rebel forces fighting on the borders. It's a war zone, not a place you'd want to live, not even if it was the place you were born.

Mina didn't talk about Iraq often, and when she did her eyes clouded over as if the past was a place she didn't want to think about. Edinburgh was her home, I know that.

And now she is gone.

'But . . . Mina is one of us!' Ross Murray says, baffled.

'She belongs here!' Chantal McKay chips in.

'They can't do this!' Lia whispers. 'Surely!'

'There must be something we can do,' I say. 'To stop it all!'

We wait for Miss McCall to tell us that we can fix this, get Mina back, but she just runs a hand through her hair and shakes her head. She tries to smile, but it's a thin smile, fragile as glass, and the class are silent, stunned. Nobody fidgets or giggles. Nobody makes a sound.

'It's not fair!' Weegie Robson bursts out, suddenly. He shoves a big pile of reading books off his desk and onto the floor, then jumps up, kicking his chair aside as he goes. He lurches across the classroom, swearing under his breath, kicking desks and chairs and finally punching his fist through a papier mâché mask of a tiger that is blu-tacked to the wall.

'Weegie!' Miss McCall says, sternly, but he just wipes a sleeve across his eyes and slams out into the corridor, and Miss McCall sighs and follows him, clutching a handful of tissues.

I notice that my mood ring has turned a dull, dark blue, as heavy as my heart. I have a feeling it will be staying that way for quite a while.

All that was a year ago, now.

If this was a story, I'd tell you that everything ended up OK. I'd say that the class got together and signed a petition and wrote letters of complaint to the authorities, and that our parents contacted their MPs to stop Mina and her family being sent back to Iraq, and that everything worked out in the end.

Well, it's not a story, it's real life, and the truth is you don't always get a happy ending. We did all of those things, but it didn't make one bit of difference. There was a flurry of headlines in the paper, just for a day or two, and then everything went quiet. We never heard from Mina or her family again.

I still wear the friendship bracelets Mina, Lia and Joe made for me on my eleventh birthday, sitting on the freshly cut grass in Princes Street Gardens, with the sound of the pipes, and the castle in the distance. It was a day I wanted to last forever, but of course, forever isn't what it seems. Sure, you can freeze the moment, keep it safe in your heart or your mind for all time, but you can't always stop bad things from happening, no matter how hard you try.

It's not that simple.

I still have the bracelets, anyhow, and I know I won't ever take them off, not even when I'm an old, old lady and they're frayed and worn, with all the colour bleached away from a lifetime of sun and rain and showers and . . . well, life.

I hope that Mina still wears hers, too.

I hope that she remembers us, and knows that we are thinking of her, and that our friendship will not fade, no matter what. Lia, Joe and I will never stop trying to find Mina. We will keep writing letters, keep asking questions, trying to make contact. And one day, when we are old enough and the war is finally over, we will go to Iraq and ask more questions, the three of us together, until we find our friend.

That's what forever means.

142

THE PORTOBELLO PIPER

JULIE BERTAGNA

The Piper seemed to blow in on a sea wind. The first anyone knew of him was the sound of bagpipes across the Portobello sands. It was a bitterly cold Tuesday morning and the sun was still yawning in thick blankets of sea mist. High on its rocky hill, Edinburgh's ancient castle seemed to float in the pearly light like a great ship lost in fog.

The Portobello Piper, as he came to be known, appeared out of the mist. Tiny tornadoes of sand whirled around his feet, like dervishes dancing to his strange music. It was almost as if, said the early morning dog-walkers, the Piper had walked right out of the sea.

Nobody ever came up with a better idea of where the Piper *did* come from. But soon enough, everyone in the city knew where he had gone – though they could hardly believe what happened, even when they saw it with their own eyes.

*

The Piper stopped at a bustling tea shop on the hill that led up from the sea towards the heart of the city. The sun had shaken off its misty blankets and the morning was warming up, so the Piper sat down at a pavement table. Sleek-suited men and women at neighbouring tables watched the stranger over their newspapers. His explosion of white hair, glittering with salt diamonds, along with the wheezing bagpipes and tattered, mismatched clothes were not what people were used to in this part of the city – and certainly not at this time in the morning.

The Piper returned their wary stares with a sea-breezy smile. But as he glimpsed the headline on one of the newspapers, his smile darkened to a frown.

The people of Edinburgh were troubled, the newspaper story said. The city streets, people complained, were overrun by strays. The homeless, the penniless and the lost, all sorts of wanderers with nowhere to go were clogging up the streets. What was worse, people said, was that no one seemed to know what to do. The city felt unsafe. So many poor and homeless on the streets made people nervous. There was even a whispered rumour that the dogs and cats of the city were disappearing: that they were being killed and roasted and eaten by homeless scavengers (though only two people were, in fact, found to have recently lost a dog or a cat; and one of those had a happy outcome when the fire brigade rescued a yowling tomcat, called Gregor, from a rooftop).

But people were worried. Something would have to be done. The homeless, it was said, were like a plague of rats in the city streets.

'Dear me,' said the Piper. He leaned towards the man in a neatly tailored suit at the table next to him. 'You look like the kind of gentleman who might know where I can find whoever is in charge of this city.'

The man frowned at the bedraggled Piper in his mismatched clothes. 'And why would you want to know that?'

The Piper tapped the newspaper that the man was folding neatly, before slipping it into his briefcase.

'This plague that's bothering the good citizens of Edinburgh,' said the Piper. 'I could help with that.'

'You?' The man gave a laugh and shut his briefcase with a snap. 'May I ask where you live? Are you an Edinburgh man?'

The Piper smiled, his eyes crinkling and glittering in the morning sun. 'Oh no,' he replied. 'I am a piper. I go where I'm needed – and you need me here.'

'Just as I thought,' said the man with a sigh. 'Another wanderer. Why don't you all go home?'

'The world is my home,' replied the Piper. 'Now, please would you take me to whoever is in charge of the city?'

The man stood up and brushed toast crumbs from his suit. His long nose wrinkled in distaste.

'Is that a *skirt* you're wearing around your neck?' he said, staring at the faded, flowery garment the Piper wore draped around his shoulders and buttoned at the neck like a cape.

'It is,' said the Piper. 'It belonged to my mother.'

With a shake of his head, the man picked up his briefcase and walked off without another word.

The Piper finished his tea in a gulp. As he put down his cup, his eyes met the dull, hungry gaze of a child. The dark, tangled mess of the child's hair made it hard to tell if it was a boy or a girl. But that was of no concern to the Piper. He offered the child the scone he had forgotten to eat, and the child grabbed it and stuffed it into a ravenous mouth. The Piper took up his bagpipes and began to play a strange, enticing music that seemed to be made of ocean winds.

The child's eyes began to sparkle. A smile spread across the sad, grubby face.

'Now,' said the Piper to the child, 'how might I help you?'

'I can help *you*,' said the child. 'I can take you to the place where the people look after the city.'

So the Piper followed the child up the hill, into the heart of the city, playing his pipes all the while. The eyes of the citizens followed him. Feet turned towards him, as people on their way to work and children on their way to school had to force themselves not to follow the spellbinding music of the Piper.

I come from a place that feels like home, said the music. *A wonderful place where you long to be; come, follow me.*

The Piper walked at the pace of the child, because the child had a limp. But the Piper didn't mind because there were such fine sights to see: the city's wide skies, rolling hills and glinting sea, the steep and twisting wynds, stately streets lined with grand buildings, and the magnificent castle on its great hill of volcanic rock.

'This is the place,' said the child, at last, leading the Piper into a grand courtyard.

The Piper looked around at the gracious buildings of the City Chambers. He took the child by the hand and they approached the door. The Piper told the doorman that he must see whoever was in charge of the city. The doorman looked at the Piper and the child with shrewd, kind eyes, but he shook his head.

'It's impossible,' he said.

The Piper thanked the doorman, but as he walked

away he began to play his bagpipes, and the music was so stirring that the doorman felt his heart would break.

'Wait a minute,' called the doorman, wiping his eyes. 'Maybe there is someone you can see.'

'It's about the city plague,' said the Piper. 'I can help.'

'I see,' said the doorman, and he led the Piper and the child up a great staircase and into a grand chamber where a group of important-looking people were sitting around an enormous, polished table.

As they entered the chamber, someone gave a loud groan. The Piper looked along the huge table and his face lit up with the brightest of smiles as he recognised the man from the tea shop.

'What are you doing here?' exclaimed the man. 'This is a private meeting for city councillors. Who let you in?'

'Is it a meeting about the city plague?' asked the Piper. 'Because if it is, I can help.'

'It just so happens it is,' said the man, 'but—'

A woman with hair as dark and shiny as the large table leaned forward to stare at the Piper. 'Are you,' she demanded, 'responsible for the music I just heard?'

'That was my pipes,' admitted the Piper.

'It was glorious,' said the woman, her eyes shining through her spectacles.

'Why don't I play some more while you have a break for tea?' said the Piper. 'There's nothing like a cup of tea and some music to help things along.'

Before anyone could object, the Piper began to play. The sound of his pipes filled the great chamber and the city councillors basked in the sound, as if it were an unexpected beam of sunshine on a dull day.

'Now,' said the Piper, with a smile, 'about this plague, as you call it. Let me tell you, I have travelled all across the world and seen the most amazing sights. I have sailed the great oceans, explored the deepest of jungles and crossed vast, scorching deserts.'

The councillors listened keenly as they sipped tea and munched buttery shortbread. So, this stranger who had burst upon them was a sophisticated, well-travelled man, not the rough vagabond that he had seemed at first.

'I have been to the most magnificent cities on earth,' continued the Piper, 'and the poorest, most wretched of places too. And I tell you, this city of yours is one of the most wonderful in the world.'

The councillors beamed at the Piper, and at each other. Of course their city was magnificent! And wasn't that just how they wanted to keep it?

'Your city is one of the richest in the world, in so many ways,' smiled the Piper. 'It is rich in wealth and in its people.'

The councillors' smiles grew even brighter. How nice that this man of the world, an exotic stranger, loved their wonderful city and its cultured citizens!

'And that is why I know,' said the Piper, 'that this city is rich enough, in all the ways that matter, to end the misery of the poor, homeless people that are its shame and disgrace.'

The city councillors gasped. One or two choked on their shortbread, which seemed to have turned to sand in their mouths.

The Portobello Piper put his arm around the shoulder of the hungry child, who was quietly stuffing his pockets with shortbread from the nearest plate. Nobody had offered any, and the councillors all had plenty, anyway.

'The worst shame of all,' said the Piper, 'is the children, like this one – the poor ones who have so little in this richest of cities.'

The councillor who had been in the tea shop stood up.

'That's all very well for you to say,' he bellowed. 'It's not an easy problem to solve. Why should we spend the hard-earned money of the good people of Edinburgh on these— these—?'

'Because of the children,' said the Piper, with a glint in his eye that was quite different from the friendly sparkle he had given the man earlier that morning. 'Because of *this* child.'

All the sunshine seemed to have left the chamber. Now, the councillors frowned gloomily and muttered among themselves.

'Listen,' said the Piper. 'I'll give you a month. When the full moon rises again, I'll be back. If you haven't done something to help these children by then, I will play a tune that you really won't like. But if you want to sleep soundly for the rest of your days, and not be forever haunted by my pipes, it's best if you put your heads together now.'

A councillor with a very red face stood up. What had been a slab of shortbread just a moment ago was now trickling through his fingers like sand.

'Get out!' shouted the councillor. 'Play all the tunes you like but you won't tell us how to run our city! You can blow your pipes till you burst for all I care.'

'Goodbye then,' said the Piper. 'I'll see you at the next full moon.'

*

One month later, the councillors were meeting again in the grand chamber.

'Well,' they said, chuckling to each other, 'we've heard not a pip from the Piper, eh?'

'It's the full moon tonight,' one of the councillors warned, 'maybe we'd better wait and see.'

Just then, the door to the chamber opened and in stepped the Piper, looking more bedraggled than ever. As he raised his hand in greeting, a small bird with feathers that were all the colours of the rainbow flew out from his sleeve and fluttered above the heads of the councillors, until it finally escaped through an open window.

'I had some work to do in the Amazon rainforest,' said the Piper. 'I had a bit of trouble getting back here in time. Now, how have you been getting along?'

'Well,' said a councillor, suddenly looking a little nervous, 'there has been such a lot to deal with that—'

'But you haven't forgotten about the children?' interrupted the Piper. 'You do remember our deal?'

'Of course we haven't forgotten about the children,' snapped the councillor. 'It's just that—'

'What exactly have you done?' said the Piper. His sea-breezy voice suddenly sounded as if he had swallowed a mouthful of sand.

'We've done lots,' said a woman councillor. 'At least, we plan to. We've talked about all kinds of things we might do . . . '

'Plan to? Might do? Talked about things?' said the Piper. 'I'm sure you mean well, but that wasn't our deal. The deal was that you were to DO something before I came back.'

'And we will. There hasn't been enough time,' said the red-faced councillor. 'We do have a whole city to run,

152

you know. This really is none of your business. Please leave or—'

'It's *everyone's* business,' said the Piper, and the door slammed behind him as he left.

*

All over the city, children looked up from whatever they were doing. A strange, thrilling music drew them to their windows and made them long for adventure, for faraway places they had never seen. They had a sudden hankering for fireworks and fizzy lemonade, for popcorn at the cinema and ice cream in the sun. The music seemed to promise hot soup on cold days, warm socks, hugs and silly jokes. It made them feel they were whooshing through the air on a swing, ripping open a present, or cycling super-fast down a hill.

But there were some who did more than listen. The forgotten children, the ones who didn't have a place that felt like home, those who were sad and scared, who didn't get much (or anything at all) for birthdays and Christmas – when those children heard the music they began to run towards it, as if the sound were a magnet they could not resist.

Out of doorways came the children, out of the wynds and steep stairways, like scatterings of winter sparrows gathering into a flock. The child with the limp heard the music too and knew at once that the Piper had kept his promise. Struggling to keep up, the child hurried to join the others in the streets. A single slab of shortbread, kept untouched as a memento of the Piper, lay deep in his pocket.

I'll eat it now, thought the child, *and then I might keep up*. But the shortbread could not be eaten. It had lain in the pocket so long it had turned hard.

The city of Edinburgh came to a standstill as people stopped to stare at the spectacle of the Portobello Piper dancing through the streets, followed by a flock of excited children. Their noise rose above the traffic as the Piper led the children, who skipped and cheered, singing and laughing, through the streets towards the castle.

Later, people said they had never seen children look so happy. It was as if all their woes and worries had dropped right away.

The setting sun and the rising full moon shone in the sky like gold and silver coins. A dusky mist had wrapped around the castle. The Portobello Piper began to climb the hill of rock which led up to the castle. To the watching citizens, the castle seemed to float in the mist like a ship about to set sail to a faraway land.

What happened next, the people of Edinburgh will never forget.

With a thunderous CRACK, a great doorway burst open in the castle rock. The Portobello Piper disappeared through the door with his flock of happy children.

The door in the rock slammed shut. The music of the Piper and the noise of the children died away. Gradually, the mist lifted. The people of Edinburgh stood as still as stones. They stared and could not believe their eyes.

The door had vanished. The Piper and the children were gone.

All night long, torch beams flashed around the city as everyone searched for the children. Every nook and cranny of the castle and its rocky hill were searched. Yet no sign was ever found of the Piper or the children who followed him through the door in the rock face.

Since that day, the citizens and their councillors have worked hard to make sure that if the Piper ever returns he will see that their city no longer ignores the poor and the homeless. Never again do they want to see a flock of forgotten children vanish through a door in the castle rock.

Yet some nights, when a bitter wind blows in from the North Sea and surges across the city to break like a wave upon the castle, people say they hear the Piper's music swirling through the streets. The citizens lock their doors and windows and close their curtains tight. They check that their children are safe and snug in bed. And they wonder about the secret smiles that light the faces of the sleeping children, as if the music of the Piper is trickling into their dreams like sand . . .

If you waken one night, listen hard, and you might hear it too – a sound that makes you glad and shivery, the way you feel as the sun yawns red and a breeze full of goosebumps spells the end of a perfect day beside the sea. Whether it really is the strange, thrilling music of the Portobello Piper, carrying echoes of happy children, who can say?

If you do hear it, maybe you, like me, will feel sure that the Piper led the children to a place that feels like home.

And maybe you have seen the man who walks with a limp through the green gardens that lie below the castle. Perhaps you see me stop and tilt my head to listen, as I lean on my walking-stick, gazing up towards the castle, wondering if the door in the rock might open again, one day.

I have never forgotten the Piper who left me behind. And he did not forget me. For just as he vanished with the other children, the slab of hard shortbread that lay in my pocket turned into a nugget of gold.

The Boy With No Name

NICOLA MORGAN

Jamie MacLeod had no name.

Not as far as his mother's new husband was concerned.

'Boy', on a good day. 'Sleekit rat', or 'useless, cow'ring, Godless runt', on a bad day.

Today was a bad day. The air in Edinburgh too hot to breathe, the stench from rot-strewn streets, skin sticky with sweat – everyone tired and tempers short. And now Jamie had made his stepfather angry – he could see it in his narrowed eyes, the creases on his sheeny forehead, the tightening of jaw muscles where his doctor's collar pressed into his flesh.

Faster than Jamie could see, a hand lashed his face, and fury swarmed through his head like bees. In a corner sat his mother, her back straight in a new dress, her belly rigid and round with another baby, her eyes tight with fear, skin grey with her own pain. And silent.

Jamie was angry with his mother then. For her silence. And for marrying this man so soon after her husband had died. The two worst days in Jamie's life: the day his father was crushed beneath the wheels of a runaway carriage, and the day, one year later, when his mother told him she was marrying again. Jamie would not say the man's name. If the man would not say Jamie's name, Jamie would not say his. Not even in his head.

And he would not call this man father. In his mind he called him the worm. It made him feel better. Not much, but a little. In a deep place, he also called him the Devil. But he feared he might go to Hell for such blasphemy. So he kept that thought very secret, hoping that even the beaky minister would not see it in his eyes when they went to the Kirk.

Jamie knew what he had done to deserve a slap. He had raised his voice to the worm. He did not know where the courage had come from. And, although he was afraid, he was not sorry.

His grandfather had disappeared. Recently, the old man's mind had been wandering in strange ways, and he had become weaker. Jamie loved him as much as ever. He loved the way he did not shout or hurry or complain about small things, the way he sometimes fell asleep during a meal, his soup tipping, or his bread falling to the floor. The way he ruffled Jamie's hair and called him a man, though Jamie was only eleven years old.

The way he sometimes talked about Jamie's two dead sisters when no one else would.

Jamie had always loved to listen to his grandfather's stories. Stories going back through  generations of his family, of war and murder and plague and cruelty. The more horrible the stories, the wider Jamie's eyes grew, and the faster his heart raced. They did not seem too real, and Jamie would listen in wonder, staring into the flames as he sat safe at the old man's feet.

One story gripped Jamie most of all. His grandfather had first told it shortly after the death of his son, Jamie's father. Whisky had taken its hold and his words slurred a little as he began. He'd often told stories of the Covenanters, but now, with watery eyes, he told his story of their defeat at Bothwell Brig. He'd been fifteen years old, the young flag-bearer, a dangerous position. He was imprisoned with hundreds of others, near Edinburgh's Greyfriars Kirk, through one freezing winter, with no shelter and a handful of bread to fight over each day.

They'd lived in an open area surrounded by walls, on which stood soldiers, ready to fire at them if they tried to escape. All for their faith it was: because they wished to worship God in their own way and not as King Charles commanded. Now his eyes were thin with remembered sadness. Jamie should have been sad for him, and he tried to imagine the cold and suffering, but he was sitting by the fire as he first heard the story, and could only wrap his arms around himself and ask for more. 'What happened then, Grandfather?'

In recent weeks, the old man had been drawn more often to this story. But in the middle of telling it, sometimes his mouth would harden and he would fall silent halfway through a sentence, and ghosts would flit across his face as, perhaps, he remembered dead friends. Last week, he'd mentioned a boy called John, a friend he said had died in prison. Then he had stopped, as though at the edge of a cliff, and had stared into the distance, forgetting that Jamie was there.

Now the old man had disappeared and the worm didn't care. 'Good riddance,' he'd said, sipping French wine. Then Jamie had told the worm he was cruel. How had he been so brave?

Or so foolish, he thought, as he ran from the room, down the two flights of stairs. It was the best floor to live on, his mother had told him: high enough above the stench, but not too high. Jamie's family was lucky. His new stepfather, after all, was a doctor, earning high fees from his customers. They still lived amongst the filth and decay of a crowded city, because everyone did, but they had a whole floor – four rooms; a maid to cook, clean and lay the fire; large windows to the back; a view of distant hills. They had moved up in the world, his mother had insisted, looking deep into his eyes as if trying to make him believe it.

Now Jamie ran out into the treacle-thick evening, airless from a heat-sodden summer's day. The man who usually slept in a deep doorway was not there yet. On the pavement lay a dead cat, and rotten meat, the ground slippery with filth.

Jamie needed to find his grandfather and he knew where to look. The old Covenanters' Prison at Greyfriars. The old man sometimes went there when he had things to think about, or on special days. More so recently. He seemed drawn there by his memories.

Jamie ran across the High Street and down crooked paths towards the Grassmarket. Greyfriars was not far beyond it. Many people were about, even at this hour, the stifling heat of their dwellings driving them outside.

There was a madness in the streets tonight, thought Jamie. As though the air was not safe to breathe. He felt uneasy. It was Midsummer's Eve, when witches and bad magic roamed, though you wouldn't see them. That woman there, laughing to herself – was she a witch? His mother always told him to be careful of such people. Though they might cure you of your illnesses, they could take you with them to the Devil, and then where would you be? Burning in Hell while the witch slipped safely back to earth between the cracks that appeared in God's world on Midsummer's Eve.

And there was a full moon, too, which had frightened his mother when she'd seen it earlier that evening. But Jamie liked the moon, its silence calm and milky. His father had loved it, too; his work had been as a night watchman, so moonlight had made it easier. Perhaps that's why his grandfather had chosen this evening to disappear: perhaps he wanted to watch the moon in peace. Well, he wouldn't mind if Jamie joined him, would he? They could talk about the worm together, maybe find a witch to put a curse on him.

Jamie ran across the Grassmarket, dodging the people packing up their stalls, lurching drunks, the street-cleaners' carts and shovels. Between the tottering buildings of Candlemaker Row he went, and towards the passageway which led to Greyfriars Kirk.

The hot night air buzzed in Jamie's head, and he stopped to wipe sweat from his eyes and gather his breath.

A clamour rose in the distance. Shouting. Screaming. A horse was approaching at a clattering gallop. A woman dragged a child from its path. Passers-by pressed themselves against the buildings. And the horse galloped by, its wide white eyes rolling.

Terrified of what? And where was the rider?

It was not long before the story followed, with the wailing of women. A man, father of five children, had been thrown from his horse and killed. The horse had been startled by a white crow, which had flown straight towards it. From the left.

A white crow, from the left, attacking a horse? It could only be an omen, warning of something terrible to come.

Then more stories, as a woman told how her neighbour's dog had given birth to a two-headed puppy, which had lived for three hours, the mother not rejecting it as she should. And could people not see the shape in the evening cloud, the shape of an upside-down cross? As they looked to the sky, some people said they could see it and fell to their knees, while others hurried away. Jamie thought at first that he could see nothing, but when he looked again, he was not sure.

In his heart, fear grew, and a wish to be home, but a fear of it. A wish to find his grandfather, but a fear of what the worm would say when they came back. Fear and wishing. Wishing to be safe, but where and what was safe? He felt safer and stronger under the Midsummer moon than he did in his own home.

Jamie ran the last short distance to the Kirkyard, slipped through the entrance and entered its shadows.

The gates would be closed soon, to keep grave-robbers out.

There hung the whole moon, cool and mysterious. But at this time of year, in Scotland, no one needed the moon to see by. Here a summer night always glowed with an eerie light.

Jamie looked around, letting the noises of the city fade behind him. Where was his grandfather? He looked towards the new memorial – that was where he often went, but no one was there. Nor near the gate to the disused prison. He peered the other way, between the gravestones. Yes! There he was! His grandfather's stooped frame and his slightly collapsed hat were unmistakeable.

Jamie ran towards him. 'Grandfather!'

Darkness shifted suddenly closer. A chill brushed his face. How strange, in air which a moment before had been heavy with heat. Jamie stopped.

He could no longer see his grandfather. He must have gone behind a gravestone. 'Grandfather! 'Tis Jamie! Wait for me!' Or perhaps he had been mistaken after all. Perhaps it was a trick of the shadows.

'Boy!'

He spun round. Two men were moving towards him. Fast. Caretakers? They must be coming to lock the graveyard. But no, not caretakers: they were dressed as soldiers, though scruffy-looking, their red coats dirty. They weren't from the City Guard either, not wearing those red coats.

'I'm searching for my grandfather!' shouted Jamie. And then he saw something that made his head spin. The men carried knives –  huge knives. Without time to think, he ran, dodging between gravestones, in the direction where he thought he'd seen his grandfather.

Darkness lurched closer again, as though someone had drawn a veil across the sky. Thunder growled in the distance. Was a storm coming? It seemed as though it might, as he ran through the clogged air. He could hear shouting behind him, but Jamie was fast and he knew he could leave them far behind.

He saw a movement behind a gravestone: the shifting of a shadow, the flick of a coat. Someone was there, he was sure. His grandfather? He ran towards it. Around the gravestone.

There was no one. He stopped, gasping for breath.

Lightning lit the graveyard and Jamie swung round. One of the men was following him still. Where was the other? Thunder crashed and Jamie jumped. Out of the corner of his eye he saw the other man coming from one side of the Kirk. Running. Jamie called out, 'Grand-father!' and changed direction, round the Kirk building and towards the south side of the graveyard. More lightning, and a yell behind him, as though one man had fallen. Jamie hoped the knife had been somewhere painful.

Thick drops of rain now began to fall, and thunder split the air again. Pressure grew in Jamie's head, throbbing in his ears. The breath was being sucked from him. His legs felt heavy. He knew one of the men was not far behind. Could Jamie get to the gate in time? Perhaps his grandfather had already left. Jamie could not wait, and yet the thought of leaving him here was . . .

'Here, boy!' A voice came from somewhere. 'Hurry!' Jamie looked up, to his right, through the rain. A boy sat on the top of a high wall, beside the gate to the Covenanters' Prison, its darkness menacing. He was beckoning to Jamie. And then Jamie saw a rope, dangling to the ground. But the wall looked high. Too high. No, he must reach the Kirkyard gates.

He sped away, twisting between gravestones. Rain blurred his eyes, plastering hair to his forehead.

No! The gates were closed. He slid to a halt. No time to think: back he ran, to where the boy still sat. Jamie grabbed the rope, felt it hold firm as he pulled himself up the wall. Like a spider, he scrambled up that sheer stone face, until he was heaving himself over the top.

'Follow me!' urged the boy, moving easily along the top of the wall, over a roof and . . . disappearing.

Jamie stopped, dropping to hands and knees to prevent himself tumbling. Lightning and thunder splintered the air. He felt himself sway, and lowered himself further, until his legs straddled the wall. The hurling rain thickened still more, running down his face. To one side, black windows stared down; to the other side, the wall surrounding the prison seemed more distant than before. He could see . . . no, he must be mistaken. The rain and the shapes of trees were playing tricks. He thought he'd seen a man standing on the wall, a soldier, musket pointing downwards. He looked again. Of course there was no soldier! Why would a soldier stand on the wall, guarding an empty prison?

From below, where the old prison lay open entirely to the sky, came a noise. A low groan. The clink of metal on stone. The shifting of bodies crushed together. A soft moaning, the sound someone might make while ill, or in the throes of a nightmare. Alert for danger, ready to move, Jamie peered through the charcoal night – for now it was fully dark, the midsummer moon no more than a memory.

At first, he could see only shadows, the shifting shapes of trees swaying beside the prison walls, a wooden sentry box, a pile of stones left by workmen building a new tomb. And then a figure, quick, small, nimble. Moving towards Jamie. The figure seemed to shout something, but his words were eaten by the sound of the rain. Jamie's heart leapt as lightning lit the sky and suddenly he could make out dark shapes on the ground, squat figures, bodies huddling together. The glinting of tiny flames, of torches perhaps. A bigger fire, with people crouched around it.

All this he saw in that one sheet of lightning. Yet, it was not possible. For when he peered again, he could see that the shapes were only patches on the earth, freshly dug, perhaps new graves being prepared. And no lights. Just the lightning playing with his vision.

'Over here!' It was the boy again. Jamie squinted through the blurring rain. The boy was at the far end of the prison, on the ground. He held a torch, its flames dancing. Jamie did not know where he had found it, but he was glad.

'How will I climb down?'

'At the end of the wall. You'll see,' the boy called back.

With care, Jamie stood up and ran to the end of the wall. At first, he could see only a sheer drop. But then he saw a workman's ladder, and within seconds he was down.

Now the boy was beckoning him towards a lean-to shelter. Jamie hurried towards it and went inside. Gasping, he wiped rain from his face and pulled his coat more tightly around him, suddenly cold. The shelter contained some simple objects: a tinder box, tools, a stool.

'Sit down. Until the rain stops.' The boy did not seem to mind the rain. His face glistened, white and wet, but he didn't wipe it away. Though he looked terribly cold, he did not shiver or pull his coat closer. It was an odd coat, Jamie thought, old-fashioned, too big. Badly torn. A black stain around one of the rips. He looked about fifteen years old. There was something strange about his eyes, too – one pale, one dark.

'I must find my grandfather,' began Jamie.

'He returned home.' The boy placed the burning torch in a holder. He seemed to be familiar with the place. Perhaps he was the son of a grave-digger.

'How do you know? Do you know my grandfather?'

'He often comes here. I see him. He was here today, before you came.'

Jamie was confused. 'He hasn't talked of you. What's your name?'

'He has not seen me. But I have seen him.'

'How do you know he's my grandfather?'

'I know. I have seen you with him. I have a message for him. I wanted to tell him today, but . . . I could not.'

'A message?' This boy knew his grandfather but his grandfather had not seen him? How could this be?

'How brave are you?' asked the boy.

'I . . . don't know. I don't believe I am very brave.' Jamie thought of how scared his stepfather made him feel. How scared he had been when both his sisters had died of typhus, and how he had shunned them while they were ill, for fear that he would become ill. And how ashamed he felt now.

'Your grandfather believes he is a coward. He is wrong. When he ran from death, he ran towards life. And that is always right. Life is a gift and must be lived fully. Tell him . . . tell him that I forgive him.'

Jamie leapt to his feet. 'What do you mean? Who *are* you? What has my grandfather done that you should forgive him?'

The boy stood his ground, unflinching. 'He will know.'

'You are crazy!' shouted Jamie. 'You do not know my grandfather! You cannot!'

The boy's eyes blazed. He held his face near the flames, and Jamie could see that one eye was blue, one deep brown. His skin was as pale as any Jamie had seen, glowing like opal in the dying torchlight. 'Tell him. And hurry. You should go now, quickly. The rain has stopped.'

Jamie looked out of the shelter. It was true. As he moved, his clothes stuck to him, cold against his skin. The air was fresher now, the heat broken by the storm, but still dark, cloud-shrouded, a thin wind sifting the leaves.

'How will I get out of this place? The gates . . . '

'Climb back up the ladder. I'll come behind you and show you another way. You need not go through the Kirkyard.'

Jamie climbed up the wooden rungs and scrambled

on to the top of the wall. The boy was just behind, though silent, not even seeming out of breath after the climb. He pointed over the edge. Jamie looked – he could see some stones protruding, the ridges of the supporting wall like steps. Below was a deserted street.

Jamie twisted himself carefully into position to climb down. As he began to find footholds and prepared to lower himself, all around the air lightened, suddenly, as if shutters had been opened. It seemed once more like summer, the night sky now a pearly blue-grey. The storm seemed strangely unreal, though his clothes were still wet.

He jumped the last few feet to the ground and looked back up. The boy's head was silhouetted against the sky, the moon watching in the background. Jamie raised his hand towards him. Whatever else the boy had done, he had helped him. What might those men have done if they'd caught him? If they thought he was a grave-robber, he would have been in great danger.

The boy raised his hand too. 'Remember to tell him.'

Jamie began to run along the pavement towards home. But, almost immediately, he stopped. Turned. Called back, 'You did not tell me your name!'

But the boy had disappeared. Only the moon stared down.

A man, very drunk, stumbled on the other side of the street. The shrill sounds of a woman shouting, a child crying, men laughing, tumbled from nearby windows:

171

the world seemed normal now. Feeling as though he had woken from a dream, Jamie hurried home, worrying about his grandfather. What if his stepfather had been cruel when he'd returned, perhaps taking revenge for Jamie's insolence?

Why had he not thought of that? Could he have put his grandfather in danger? Fear gripped him and he ran, sure-footed on the rough ground, nipping round the corners, breathless, as if chased by something invisible.

There was the High Street, the tottering buildings leaning over it. There, its mouth narrow and black, was the tiny close where he lived. There was the bundle of rags – the young man who spent most nights in that doorway. Jamie yelped as he scraped his elbow on the stonework when he turned into the close too fast. A white rat scuttled, ghostlike, in front of him, disappearing into a hole in the wall. Jamie shuddered. Midsummer madness was still in the air.

And there was the entrance to his stair. Dark and hot, tunnel-like.

He paused, and then leapt up the wooden stairs, two at a time.

Jamie flung open the door of his dwelling. He stood there, breathing heavily. There was the familiar, horrible smell of the worm's home. His old home had smelt of firewood and food. This one smelt of bitter herbal tinctures and oatmeal poultices and wet bandages and whisky. The doctor was always making new potions, hiding away in the room he used for himself, sometimes shouting orders for more water and soap and salt and spirits.

Jamie's mother rushed from a doorway, looking startled when she saw him. Her hand flew to her mouth, her eyes red-rimmed, thin trails of hair curling damply on her forehead.

'Oh, Jamie! Where were you?'

'Where's Grandfather?'

'Oh, Jamie! He was taken ill!'

'Where? Let me see him!'

Then came the worm's voice. 'Keep the boy away! This is no place for a child.'

But Jamie ran towards the voice, through the door. His grandfather lay on a bed, his eyes closed. An oil lamp burned beside him, another on a table. The worm stood at the foot of the bed, anger on his face as he saw Jamie.

'Get out of here! What did I tell you?' The worm turned to Jamie's mother, scowling.

But Jamie stared at his grandfather, drinking in what he saw, trying to make sense. It was almost impossible to see the old man's chest move, but moving it was, slowly. The face was soft, dribble coming from the corner of his mouth. And then the eyes opened and a small sound came, along with a twist of a half smile. One hand beckoned to Jamie.

Jamie looked at his mother, and at her husband. Then he walked towards the bed. And no one stopped him.

Jamie took his grandfather's hand. It lay limp in his. The old man moved his other hand and took Jamie's. This hand was strong, alive.

'I went to find you. At Greyfriars Kirk. But you had gone. A boy told me. He seemed to know who you were but I . . .'

The old man's eyes opened wide. Or, Jamie noticed, one eye only, for the other seemed weak, half closed. He tried to speak but his words were faint at first.

'What is it, Grandfather?'

'Leave your grandfather, boy. He needs to rest.'

Jamie turned to the worm and spoke, calmly, politely. 'Please, Sir. I will speak with my grandfather.' Inside, he could not untangle his grief and anger. Outside, he was strong.

His stepfather looked at though he might strike Jamie again, but a doctor is respectful when death is watching. He shrugged his shoulders as though he cared nothing. Jamie turned back to the old man and listened to his words.

'Wha' boy?'

'A strange boy. Older than I.'

'Wha' name?'

'He did not say his name.'

And then came a word which at first Jamie could not make out, so full of emotion was the old man's voice. Three times his grandfather tried to say something, and three times Jamie strained to hear.

The old man pulled Jamie closer, gripping with one hand. Then he took his hand from Jamie's arm and pointed with a wavery finger at Jamie's face. At his eyes.

Eyes!

'He had one blue eye and one brown,' said Jamie.

The hand fell back. The eyes closed. Tears squeezed between them.

His eyes opened again and now there was fear in them. But the words came more strongly, as if desperately. 'When you see him, tell him I am sorry.'

Jamie remembered the boy's message. He was about to tell his grandfather but the old man was speaking again. 'I ran away, Jamie. You know the story, of our defeat. But I did not tell you the end. I ran away.' He shook his head, pain in his eyes.

'But you were in the prison, grandfather. You told me.'

His grandfather struggled to produce the words, and it was not easy for Jamie to hear them clearly. But he understood well enough. And the more the old man tried, the clearer the words became.

'Aye, but I was freed. I betrayed them, Jamie, lad. This

I did not tell you. I was . . . too ashamed. A soldier promised our freedom if we would reject the oath we swore to God. John refused. I told him God did not wish us to die, but he cursed me for my treachery. He was my friend. But we fought, Jamie.' The strong hand was clenched tight as a clam, motionless on the blanket.

'What happened then, Grandfather?' This was like one of the stories he loved to hear. And yet, it was not like that. It was real, and the pain in his grandfather's eyes was horribly real.

The old man's voice was slurred but his meaning was clear. 'The soldiers freed those of us who agreed. John did not. Nor did he look at me again. The next day, many of them were executed. I did not see John die, but I know he did. How he must have hated me.'

The old man's body loosened, exhausted. He closed his eyes again. Sadness was etched in his face, in the wrinkles around his eyes, in the drooping of his mouth.

Jamie was confused. 'But who is the boy? How does he know about this?'

'John had one blue eye and one brown.'

Jamie's thoughts whirled. He could not bear to think what this meant, or to believe it. This was surely some story of his grandfather's. This was not real.

The old man's breathing was becoming slower.

Then Jamie remembered. 'He forgave you, grandfather. He told me to tell you. He said . . . ' What was it? Something about life? And then Jamie heard the boy's voice. And he repeated the words as he heard them in his head. 'Life is a gift and must be lived fully.'

His grandfather's eyes opened, the one good eye more than the other. He gripped Jamie's hand. Passion entered his voice. 'Did he say that, Jamie? Did he?'

'He did.' Jamie felt the hand clench and unclench.

After a few moments' silence, during which the old man stared into the distance, he smiled and looked at Jamie, his gaze watery and bright. 'I did live life fully, Jamie, lad. And you must do that too. *Never* throw your life away. Do what you can with it but never throw it away. Think of this: if I had stayed with John and the others, you would never have been born. Your life is a gift, too, Jamie, lad. My gift to you.'

'Jamie! Come now. Your grandfather must rest.' His mother's hand was on his shoulder.

'Do as your mother says, Jamie,' said the worm. Jamie looked at him. The worm had called him by his name! How strange it sounded, coming from a worm.

Later that night, his grandfather's life slipped away. His mother told him in the morning, her own eyes red, and she put her arms around him, gripping him to her, so that Jamie felt the kicking of the new life in her belly. He clung to her for a few extra moments. Later, when no one was looking, Jamie cried. He cried for the passing of such a good man, but he cried too for lost stories, for his father, for John, for murderous soldiers. And then he dried his eyes and did not cry again.

Now Jamie MacLeod had a name. But that was not the most important thing. What his stepfather or anyone else did could not matter. Jamie had the gift of life, and only his own actions mattered: living. Living life fully. And his grandfather had not only given him that. He had also given him hope.

Jamie looked out of the wide window that morning. He saw the glittering spires of churches, the distant hills, his world spread out in front of him. And hanging above them, in the brightness of an early sky, a papery moon, watching silently as always. Compared to all this, this whole world of his, he felt small, and yet not as small as before.

Authors' Biographies

JONATHAN MERES

I was born in Nottingham, and left school at sixteen to join the merchant navy. I spent the next seven years sailing around the world. I left the sea to become a rock star, but became an ice-cream van driver instead. After that I got a job as an actor. Like you do.

Since then, I've acted in children's theatre, as well as on the telly and in movies. I was even a comedian for ten years. I called myself Johnny Immaterial. I've got awards to prove it!

My proper job's writing though. I've written lots of things for TV and radio, as well as picture books and books for older children and teenagers, such as the *Yo! Diary!* series, *Love Dad*, *Fame Thing*, *Clone Zone* and *Diary of a Trainee Rock God*.

I never actually *meant* to live in Edinburgh. It just kind of happened. I'm glad it did, though. From one side of my house I can see Arthur's Seat. From the other, I can see the Pentland hills. As I write these words, I look out of my study window and see a number 33 bus go past. I couldn't imagine living anywhere else.

Visit Jonathan's website at www.jonathanmeres.co.uk.

ELIZABETH LAIRD

Travel has always been in my blood: I was born in New Zealand, but grew up in London. Since then, I've lived in many parts of the world, including Ethiopia, Malaysia, Iraq and Lebanon, and my feet just keep on itching! I now flit between London and Edinburgh. I love Edinburgh because of the smell of sea, the lure of the hills, the buzz of the streets, and the ghosts of my ancestors on every corner.

My books include contemporary fiction and historical fiction, as well as shorter novels and picture books for younger children. Some of the stories are set overseas, in Kurdistan, Ethiopia, Lebanon and Pakistan, and some are set in Britain, and deal with the problems and concerns of young people growing up here today.

I've been lucky enough to win many awards, including the Scottish Arts Council Children's Book of the Year, and have been shortlisted for the Costa Awards, the Blue Peter Awards, and five times for the Carnegie Medal. My books are translated into more than fifteen languages around the world.

Visit Elizabeth's website at www.elizabethlaird.co.uk.

KEITH GRAY

When I was at primary school I was definitely the best tree-climber in the school, but probably one of the worst readers too. I avoided books. There were so many trees where I grew up that I didn't really have time for reading. But I soon realised that tree-climbing wasn't going to turn out to be a proper job, no matter how good I was at it, and my friend gave me a copy of *The Machine Gunners* by Robert Westall. It was this book that instantly made me want to become a writer.

I've now written several award-winning books for teenagers and young people, including *The Runner*, *Malarkey* and *Ostrich Boys*. Recently, I had the fantastic experience of being Scottish Book Trust's first ever Virtual Writer in Residence. I live in Edinburgh with my girlfriend and our parrot, and we have some brilliant trees very close by . . .

Visit Keith's website at www.keith-gray.com.

JOHN FARDELL

I've been a cartoonist for longer than I've been an author. My comic strips and cartoons have appeared in *Viz*, the *Herald*, the *Independent* and *The List*, among others. I also did quite a lot of work in puppet theatre during the 1990s.

So far, I've written and illustrated two children's adventure novels, *The Seven Professors of the Far North* and *The Flight of the Silver Turtle*, with a third – *The*

Secret of the Black Moon Moth – coming out in January 2009. I've also just written and illustrated my first picture book, *Manfred the Baddie*, which is currently shortlisted for the first Roald Dahl Funny Prize.

I was brought up near Bristol, and have lived in Edinburgh since 1992. Like many writers and illustrators, I find Edinburgh fires my imagination. It's such a multi-layered city, in every sense. To me, it seems the ideal starting point for stories of eccentric inventors, awe-inspiring secrets and extraordinary adventures.

My wife and I have lived in various parts of the city over the years. These days, we live in Corstorphine, with our two sons. I work in what used to be the garage, on the side of the house.

VIVIAN FRENCH

I've been an actor, a story-teller, and now I'm a writer. My first books for children were published in 1990, and since then I've written over 200 books, including picture books, non-fiction, modern fairy tales for fluent readers and novels for teenagers. I'm very lucky to be amongst the most borrowed authors in UK libraries – my books were borrowed over half a million times last year. Libraries are AMAZING; I'm a massive fan.

I've been shortlisted for many awards: recently I won the Stockton Children's Book of the Year for *The Robe of Skulls*. I've visited schools from Orkney to Oklahoma, and have been writer in residence at festivals all over the world – but I'm happiest when I'm at home in Edinburgh. One day, I was standing at my local bus stop, and an elderly Morningside lady asked me what I did. 'I write books for children,' I said. 'Oh,' came the reply, 'you're in the right place, then. Edinburgh's got stories in her bones and her stones.' That's so true – and I love it!

Visit Vivian's website at www.vivianfrench.co.uk.

ALISON FLETT
I was born and bred in Edinburgh, and to me it's the most beautiful city in the world. I've been living in Orkney for nine years now, but whenever I come back to Edinburgh it's like coming home. It feels like I've put my slippers on when the train pulls into Waverley and I see the castle: the same castle I saw from my bedroom window in Leith when I was wee.

The great thing about Edinburgh is its contrasts: there are beautiful old buildings right next to fantastic new ones; you can stand on North Bridge with the traffic buzzing behind you and look out at the calm blue of the North Sea. However, some contrasts are not so good. Edinburgh is a very wealthy city, and yet many people who live there struggle to make ends meet, so it's great to see a project committed to changing that.

I don't imagine children are very interested in literary awards, so I won't tell you that I won the Belmont Prize for children's poetry and the Hi-Arts short story competition. Neither will I mention being shortlisted for the *Scotsman*/Orange Prize and the Saltire First Book of the Year Award.

ALISON PRINCE

I grew up in South London during the war. We were bombed rather a lot, but I enjoyed collecting shrapnel. I got into writing accidentally on a TV series called *Joe*, followed by *Trumpton* and stories for *Jackanory*. I've now written over forty books, and I was thrilled to win the Guardian Children's Fiction Award in 1996 for a Robin Hood story set in modern Glasgow, *The Sherwood Hero*.

My first baby was born in Edinburgh. During the months before he arrived, I walked for miles all over the city. Walked through the Old Town, up and down the stairs and wynds; down the hill from the Castle and across Princes Street; along beside the tumbling Water of Leith; and round to places where the wind blew through long grass. I climbed up high, and stared out over the docks and the sea. Later, I worked in schools further out in the city, and saw how different it was there from the grand buildings of Waverley. I remember feeling quite lonely in Edinburgh, and perhaps that's why the boy in my story is absolutely alone (at the beginning, anyway), except for the voice in his head. I live on the Isle of Arran now, and love it, but I still come back to Edinburgh from time to time.

Visit Alison's website at www.alisonprince.co.uk.

CATHY CASSIDY

I've always wanted to be an author, so when my first children's book, *Dizzy*, was published in 2004 it was a real dream come true. More books followed . . . *Indigo Blue*, *Driftwood*, *Scarlett*, *Sundae Girl*, *Lucky Star*, *Gingersnaps* . . . and the ideas keep coming! I live in the Galloway country-side with my husband, kids, a bunch of unruly pets, and a tepee in the garden. I'm not a Scot by birth, but Scotland has been home for most of my adult life – it has the wildest countryside, the coolest cities, the best festivals!

Edinburgh is always buzzing with energy, excitement and possibilities – it was an honour to write something for *Our City*.

Visit Cathy's website at www.cathycassidy.com.

JULIE BERTAGNA

My first memory of Edinburgh is of a fairytale city with a castle, grand old streets, and shops full of tartan dolls and sticks of pink rock. The big castle was gloomy and scary (I was only four), but I was entranced by what seemed to be a Cinderella Castle, like the one in my storybook, on Princes Street. So I whined until I got my own Cinderella Castle – a small, plastic model of the Scott Monument. Even now, when I step off the train from Glasgow, it seems strangely like something out of a fairytale, stuck bang in the middle of Princes Street.

I like to write exciting, unusual, extraordinary stories, often about outsiders trying to find their place in the world. The OneCity Trust tackles things close to my heart. My first book, *The Spark Gap*, was about homeless runaways in Glasgow. *Exodus* and *Zenith* are epic stories of young survivors desperate for a home on a future, flooded Earth. It's been wonderful to win awards for my books, but the best thing is hearing from so many passionate young readers all over the world.

Visit Julie's website at www.juliebertagna.com.

NICOLA MORGAN

You could say my childhood was a little different from most. Until I was eleven, I lived in a boys-only boarding school. When I went to a girls' boarding school, they were strangely unimpressed by my tree-climbing and weapon-making skills.

I became a teacher, but all the time I was trying to be a writer. It took me many years to get published, but now I write books full-time (when I'm not doing school talks or festivals throughout the UK and in Europe). I've won some awards, including the Scottish Arts Council Children's Book of the Year Award for *Sleepwalking*, and I was shortlisted for the Aventis Science Prize for *Blame My Brain*. I'm also proud of having invented Brain Cake™, designed to power your brain. (Recipe on my website!)

Edinburgh is now my home. Its streets, history and people often inspire my work, such as the gory *Fleshmarket*, and my next novel, *Deathwatch*, about a girl being stalked by an insect-collector. Be careful when

186

you're out and about in Edinburgh: you could end up in my next book . . .

Visit Nicola's website at www.nicolamorgan.co.uk.

JAMES MACKENZIE (*Introduction*)
James Mackenzie is best known as the star of BBC Scotland's *Raven*, the BAFTA Award-winning children's adventure game show.

Visit the *Raven* website at www.bbc.co.uk/cbbc/raven.